IF ANDY WARHOL
HAD A GIRLFRIEND

IF ANDY WARHOL
HAD A GIRLFRIEND

ALISON PACE

BERKLEY BOOKS, NEW YORK

THE BERKLEY PUBLISHING GROUP
Published by the Penguin Group
Penguin Group (USA) Inc.
375 Hudson Street, New York, New York 10014, USA
Penguin Group (Canada), 10 Alcorn Avenue, Toronto, Ontario M4V 3B2, Canada
(a division of Pearson Penguin Canada Inc.)
Penguin Books Ltd., 80 Strand, London WC2R 0RL, England
Penguin Group Ireland, 25 St. Stephen's Green, Dublin 2, Ireland (a division of Penguin
Books Ltd.)
Penguin Group (Australia), 250 Camberwell Road, Camberwell, Victoria 3124, Australia
(a division of Pearson Australia Group Pty. Ltd.)
Penguin Books India Pvt. Ltd., 11 Community Centre, Panchsheel Park, New Delhi –
110 017, India
Penguin Group (NZ), Cnr. Airborne and Rosedale Roads, Albany, Auckland 1310,
New Zealand (a division of Pearson New Zealand Ltd.)
Penguin Books (South Africa) (Pty.) Ltd., 24 Sturdee Avenue, Rosebank, Johannesburg 2196,
South Africa

Penguin Books Ltd., Registered Offices: 80 Strand, London WC2R 0RL, England

This book is an original publication of The Berkley Publishing Group.

This is a work of fiction. Names, characters, places, and incidents either are the product of
the author's imagination or are used fictitiously, and any resemblance to actual persons, living
or dead, business establishments, events, or locales is entirely coincidental.

Copyright © 2005 by Alison Pace.
Cover images by AXB Group. Cover design by Rita Frangie.
Back cover photo of woman with dogs by Darryl Estrine for Getty Images.
Text design by Tiffany Estreicher.

First edition: February 2005

Library of Congress Cataloging-in-Publication Data

Pace, Alison.
    If Andy Warhol had a girlfriend / Alison Pace.— 1st ed.
        p. m.
    ISBN 0-425-20024-8 (Berkley trade pbk.)
        1. Women art dealers—Fiction. 2. Women travelers—Fiction. 3. New York
(N.Y.)—Fiction. 4. Artists—Fiction. I. Title.
    PS3566.A24I38   2005
    813'.54—dc22   2004055087

PRINTED IN THE UNITED STATES OF AMERICA

10   9   8   7   6   5   4   3   2   1

FOR MY PARENTS

I'd like to extend a very special thank you to Joanna Schwartz, a never-ending source of inspiration, encouragement, and joy for any and all undertakings.

I'm *really,* really grateful to Allison McCabe for her terrific editing, thoughtful guidance, and excellent sense of humor. Tremendous thanks also to Alanna Ramirez and everyone at Berkley for all their efforts.

For years of friendship and for reading this book as it was being written, thanks to Sarah Melinger, Cynthia Zabel, Jennifer Geller, Christine Ciampa, and Sandy Ferris. Sorry about all the peanut butter cups.

For endless enthusiasm along the way, many thanks to Peter Aaron, Adam Bram, Norma Drelich, Betty Ferm, Meredith Kaback, Alfred Levitt, Ross Meltzer, Susan Menconi, Francis Tucci, Joe Veltre, Caroline Wallace, and Rebecca Weisberg.

To my wonderful parents, Jane and Michael Pace: Grazie mille for your unwavering support, love, and pride. This would have been impossible without you.

"They always say time changes things,
but you actually have to change them yourself."
—Andy Warhol

PROLOGUE

AS SMOOTH AS
TENNESSEE WHISKEY

"People should fall in love with their eyes closed."
—Andy Warhol

I didn't always hate daisies.

I didn't always see them as grim omens of death. But that was before I met Jack.

The first time I saw him he was sitting across from me at a long table in an Italian restaurant on Second Avenue. It isn't there anymore. It was on one of those blocks in New York where nothing is able to take root; every few months you notice Pomodoro has changed to Turkish or Thai or something. I really can't remember the name of the restaurant. I can't remember what I ate either. But I will always remember everything else.

"I'm Jack."

He was a beautiful man. Before he even spoke a word I thought how he must always turn heads. I had butterflies in my stomach. "Hi," I said, and I was no longer twenty-seven. I had just returned to eleven.

"Hi . . . and what do people call you?"

"Oh, uh—" *Oh, God.* "Jane."

"Hi, Jane, pleasure to meet you."

"Hi."

He was the best-looking man I had ever seen in real life. To put it in perspective, back then my friend Kate and I had a foolproof test we gave ourselves to determine if we should bother going on a second date with a guy: "Can you see him with his shirt off?" we'd ask each other. If the answer was yes, you'd go out again. I wanted to take Jack's shirt and hide it somewhere he would never find it.

"Well, Jane," he said, "I am going to the bar to have a smoke. Want to join me?"

He said it slowly, almost drawling. You could hear his voice kind of catching on the *J* sounds in *Jane* and *join*. Maybe he was from Texas? I thought of Lyle Lovett and all the songs he had written for Julia Roberts—but then didn't he write all those songs after they broke up? I stopped thinking about *Long Tall Texan* and thought instead of the real, live, long, tall, possible Texan across the table from me. I watched his khakis unfold and get taller. I didn't want the feeling I had from being around him to go away.

Want to join me?

Two years. That's how long it had been since I'd last had a cigarette. *I could have just one,* I thought, *one won't destroy all the nonsmoking effort of the past two years.* And technically, it wasn't two years anyway. There was Kate's wedding. I'd had two cigarettes that night. Actually, I'd had four. But how could I not? My best friend was getting married and moving away, far away, to Miami. Surely, a few cigarettes that emotional night of all nights does not belie a shameless, hopeless addiction? And I didn't go back to smoking after that. So I could have the occasional cigarette, and still not return shamefully to the official "I am-a-smoker-standing-on-the-street-corner-like-a-junkie-or-a homeless-person" kind of addiction. I stood up to go with Jack, who was maybe from Texas and who was definitely for me.

He picked up my wine and carried it to the bar.

A gentleman.

This was why I was still single. I had been fortunate enough to arrive unencumbered, without baggage, without a messy relationship to get over, at the doorstep of The Perfect Man. I climbed on to a bar stool next to him. At that moment I *knew*. I knew it was the love at first sight I had always believed in. I asked him for his last name.

"Davis," he told me.

Davis.

Jane Davis. Mr. and Mrs. Jack Davis.

He pulled out a pack of Marlboro Lights. My beloved Marlboro Lights, sweet long-lost friends! Of course he would smoke Marlboro Lights. I hated the harsh-and-dirty-truck-driver appeal of Marlboro Reds, loathed the I-listened-to-the-Dead-in-college cachet of Camel Lights. But he, he simply had nice, white Marlboro Lights.

True Love.

He smiled at me and the entire world stopped. It was a

smile I would see many times and it would have the same effect every time, no matter what else was happening. It was a magic smile. It would knock down anything in its path. He would smile and everything inside me would feel warm and soft. He was able to get this reaction from almost everyone he met. It was a gift. Jack could look at you, no matter who you were, and make you feel like what you had to say, what you had to offer, were the most important things in his world. It made you want to give him yourself. It made you want to give him everything.

"What do you do, Jane?"

"I work at an art gallery called Dick Reese," I answered.

People who knew enough to not major in art history don't always know what I am talking about when it comes to my work. Everyone has heard of Goldman Sachs and Condé Nast, but when you tell someone you work at a gallery, no one without an active interest in art has ever heard of it.

He exhaled and looked directly at me. "Contemporary art, right?"

Oh. My. God.

1

A GIRLFRIEND IN THEORY ONLY?

"Everybody has a different idea of love."
—Andy Warhol

The Fall Art Fair
New York, New York

Two years after that night, I couldn't find my favorite pair of black pants. They weren't at the cleaners and they weren't in my apartment. It is so hard to find a really good pair of black pants, and this pair made by Theory was the best I ever had. I wore them all the time. I realized I had left them at Jack's. He was in San Francisco on a business trip and I hadn't heard from him since he'd left. I didn't want to call and bother him about something as trivial as *pants*.

I didn't have to call him, though; I could get the pants via Jeremy.

Jeremy was Jack's roommate from college, and was staying at Jack's while he looked for an apartment it seemed he might never find. Jeremy was a really nice guy. He told me I looked pretty like he meant it each time he saw me. I had been meaning to schedule dinner with him. I could pop over, retrieve the black pants, and make the invitation.

The Night I Went to Get the Pants was oppressively hot.

We'd had a spring in New York that felt like summer, and now in August it was over a hundred degrees every day and the world was a giant hair dryer blowing in your face. I felt wilted when I arrived at Jack's apartment. Jeremy let me in and told me my shirt was a nice color.

"Hi, Jeremy," I said. "Thanks!"

He told me my hair looked great, and asked if I had gotten it cut.

"No, it's the same." I said. "Look, I'm here to get my pants, but I've got the whole night free." I headed to Jack's bedroom, where I had a drawer in the middle of his dresser, as I asked, "So, want to grab dinner with me?" I was sure my black pants would be in that drawer, along with these gray pants from the Gap I liked to wear around the apartment and my favorite long-sleeved T-shirt. Someone had given it to Jack, but it was too small for him so he gave it to me.

Strangely they weren't there.

No black pants, no loungey pants, and no favorite T-shirt either.

Where were they? Top drawer? No. The top drawer was socks and personal things. As tempting as it was to look in *that* drawer, the one time I did I found pictures of Jack's girl-friend before me, and her very big boobs bummed me out and I had to confess to him. *Bottom drawer?* The bottom drawer was just old shirts. I started looking around the room. His bed was unmade. *Maybe I should make it for him? But didn't I make it Friday morning before we left?*

I looked on top of the dresser. Jack kept this really nice picture of us on top. It was taken a month after we started dating; we had been at the beach for the weekend. We were both tan and smiling—in a way, we looked alike. We both had the exact same color light brown hair and light brown eyes. And we were almost the same shade of tan. It was the very first summer of our romance. I always thought that im-age would get us through whatever winters we would have to face.

The picture wasn't there.

I tried not to be shaky as I went into the living room, where Jeremy offered me a beer. I reminded myself that there could be a logical explanation for everything. I looked around the living room. I looked at all the picture frames on the mantel. *Maybe he moved our picture to the living room?* There wasn't any picture of me in the living room. *Where the fuck was the damn fucking happy picture?*

I heard Jeremy ask if I'd found my pants as all the edges of the room started to go blurry.

"I couldn't find them. Jack's room is kind of a mess," I lied.

"I have no idea what J.D. does in there," Jeremy said as he stood looking at the bottle in my hand and not my eyes.

What? Why would he say something like that? The

blurry thing was still happening and then I saw the daisies. Next to all of the picture frames on the mantel, excluding of course one with a picture of me in it, I saw a vase holding a bouquet of daisies. *Did Jeremy buy Jack daisies? Do guys buy flowers for themselves sometimes?*

"Jeremy, you brought some daisies to brighten the place up?" I asked in a voice that didn't sound anything like my own to me.

"No. I didn't buy those."

Now Jeremy looked at the daisies instead of me. The words hung in the thick, wavy air. I stared at the daisies. Each one was a person who had no idea who they had been with for two whole years. No. I. Didn't. Buy. Those.

This couldn't be happening.

I had waited so long to find him. He made me laugh. He made me happy. He made me feel safe. He made me feel loved. He knew everything about me. He was my best friend. Yes, we had broken up for four months while he figured out what he wanted, but he figured it out and he wanted *me*. He wanted to get married. We were going to get married! It was a plan. We walked by the church on Twelfth Street *talking* about our wedding! When people would ask, "Who are you?" I was going to tell them, "I am Mrs. Jane Davis. I used to work at the Dick Reese Gallery but now I stay home with the kids, Blake and Lynne, and I am a Really Good Mom and a Very Happy Wife. The kids are perfect little light brown-eyed angels. They just love the Volvo so much they hardly complain about the weekend drives to Connecticut."

On the mantel, next to the devil daisies, there was a small, white card.

I wished that Jeremy would do something. I wished he would tell me how he had been joking, that yes he had taken himself down to the bodega on the corner to buy daisies. *Please, Jeremy, you can say that.* I would have believed him. I would have believed anything. I wanted so, so badly to believe anything other than that Jack had had someone there, someone he bought flowers for. *Could the card be for me?* Maybe an e-ticket confirmation number was written on it, and I was to fly out to San Francisco for a romantic vacation? We could rent a convertible and drive to Napa; we could drink wine at the Auberge du Soleil. Maybe he was going to propose? I took the card from the mantel. Just because I couldn't find my picture or my pants, and just because, come to think of it, he had been acting like such a jerk before he left, to think something so terrible had gone on . . . I read the message.

Thanks for the cheeseburgers. Thanks for a perfect second date.
　　　　　—Daisy Crowe (that's Crowe with an e.)

I will never be able to look a daisy in the eye again. In that moment I knew with absolute certainty that for the rest of my life, whenever I saw a daisy I would remember how everything that I had believed in turned out not to be true. He was my best friend in the world, he listened to everything I said, he supported me and believed in me and made me feel like the sun shone only for me. He was going to take care of me forever.

And none of it was true.

Thanks for the cheeseburgers. Thanks for a perfect second date.
        —Daisy Crowe (that's Crowe with an e.)

Jack had a balcony and a grill. On our second date, he invited me for dinner and made me a cheeseburger. I had told him it was my favorite food. *I will from this day forward,* I thought, *be a vegetarian.* And cheeseburgers? Plural? Did she eat two? What was she, a tall, long-legged, lacrosse-playing blonde who could eat whatever she wanted and never gain a pound? And what was the "e" clarification at the end? Was it a private joke? They already had a private joke? Had he brought Daisy daisies and given her a card with Crowe spelled like it was, a black, creepy, omen of death?

A pack of Jack's cigarettes were on the coffee table. I took one. It didn't matter. I was standing on the brink, looking over into the abyss and if that cigarette was going to keep me from falling over, I was going to have it. I was going to have the whole pack. I can't remember how long I stood there and I can't remember anything Jeremy said. I know I lit another cigarette standing there.

Eventually I left and walked across Central Park even though it was dark.

I was never going to the Upper West Side again. There are those people who will tell you, as if it is divine truth, that there is no reason to ever go to the Upper West Side. I was to join their ranks, effective immediately. I came out of the park and started walking south. I stopped in front of the Metropolitan Museum, looked at the flags hanging from the roof, and tried to ignore the fact that the Stanhope Hotel was only one block away. We used to have Bloody Marys at the Stanhope on Sundays. I would never be able to look at that building again. I realized this was going to happen everywhere.

Everywhere I loved, every place that had made New York feel like home to me, had in some way been shared with Jack. Slowly, I walked halfway up the steps of the museum and then turned around and sat down. I thought about a magnet on my refrigerator. It said, "Art Can't Hurt You." There were not enough cigarettes in the world to take care of my pain.

I lit one.

I was a junkie. I was a homeless person.

2

THE SCHNAUZERS LOVE
ARTICHOKES

"Machines have less problems.
I'd like to be a machine."
—Andy Warhol

The next day I stayed in bed and smoked cigarettes and drank chocolate milk and concentrated on the tears running over my nose and onto the pillow that had been Jack's. Kate called to see if I wanted to talk. I had called her late in the night, my very best friend, and sobbed that it was over and that there were daisies. She didn't completely understand but she was good enough not to ask questions, and she stayed on the phone with me as my breathing slowed and I got that hiccup thing between breaths.

"No. Katie, I don't. I can't."

"I just wish I could see you. It's so hard to be in Miami

when I want to come over and make sure you are okay. Maybe I should get a flight?"

I wished so badly that I could say, "Yes, fly to New York." I wanted her to lie in bed with me and talk to me and make me see the world through anyone else's eyes but my own. But I couldn't. Kate had a baby.

"No, I am awful company. You should stay with the baby," I told her.

"Okay, well, we are just going to talk on the phone a lot then. Until you are okay. What are you doing now? Have you called anyone? Where is Elizabeth? What about Victor? Did you tell the gallery that you are sick?"

"Nothing. I haven't called anyone. I don't want to tell anyone what happened. I called the gallery this morning and told Clarissa my back went out." I exhaled.

"Jane, are you *smoking?* Look I'm not going to bother you, and you do whatever it is you need to do to get through this. So I understand if you are lying in bed all day smoking cigarettes, but I hope that you aren't."

"Okay."

"Janie, " she said firmly, "it will all be okay. He's a jerk, really he is. And I'm not just saying that to make you feel better. I never trusted him. You must simply never talk to Jack again and you will be fine soon."

Duh! Duh! I wasn't ever going to talk to Jack again! But I wasn't going to be fine soon. I wasn't going to be fine ever. I was going to stay in bed. "Thanks. I will call you real soon. Promise."

"Okay, I'm here. Hang tough!"

Kate is a born cheerleader. I hung up the phone and thought about what she had said, about never talking to Jack again. Even though there was Daisy Crowe with an *e,* the thought of never hearing his voice, never talking to him or seeing him or touching him ever again seemed a far worse fate than being cheated on. I considered having a modern new-millennium romance, where he could do things like that and they wouldn't hurt me and we would sweep it all under the rug.

Then I took a swig of NyQuil and went back to sleep until the next day.

The second day, I made myself get out of bed and look in the mirror. I stared at my reflection, taking inventory of all the things Jack didn't want anymore. My height, always below average at five-foot-four, suddenly seemed Lilliputian. My weight, firmly in the middle of the ten-pound arc I've ridden throughout my life, taking me from people telling me I looked thin, to them not looking at me as if I'd said anything strange when I announced I was on a diet, suddenly seemed way too high. My hair, once the same color as Jack's, now looked mousy and dull. I wondered if I'd ever look at myself and see anyone other than someone who had been forgotten.

I called the gallery to tell them my back had not gotten any better and that sadly, regretfully, I was going to stay at home again, but to please call me if they needed anything. I got back into bed for a quick nap but the phone started ringing almost immediately.

"Hello."

"Jane. It's Elizabeth. Are you okay? I talked to Kate and she told me that you and Jack broke up. I'm sorry. Can I bring you anything? Do you need anything?"

I need a time machine. I could go back to the night I met Jack and decline his invitation to smoke a cigarette. But what I really want is to go back to when he met Daisy Omen of Death and make sure he doesn't. "No, but thanks. I just want to spend a day at home with a movie or something and then I'll be okay."

"Jane, you'll tell me if you need anything? Craig and I are right down the street."

"Thanks." *Exactly what I want to picture right now, you and your fiancé.* "I'll call you soon."

I made sure the shades were as closed as could be and looked forward to sleeping for the entire day. I felt momentarily cheered by the possibility of sleeping for the entire week. Or maybe for the next six months. The phone rang again. *Damn it all to hell.*

"Hello."

"Janie. It's Victor. Your back okay?"

Victor Hanrahan works with me. Despite having to toil together under adverse conditions, or maybe because of it, our years of servitude at the Dick Reese Gallery have made us close friends. Victor is brightness and cheerfulness personified—his looking at a flower could make it bloom. I believe firmly that in another life, a life in which the romance gods and I got on a bit better, Victor and I were happily married. Sadly for me, in this life, he, as they say, plays for the other team.

"Oh, Victor. My back is fine. It's actually—uh, it's actually Jack and I broke up." I gulped through the last two words.

"Oh, Janie. I'm sorry. I love you, sweetheart, I do. And that golf-playing Texan will never have anyone half as good as you." He paused for a minute, maybe to be sure I had really heard him, and then asked, "Do you need anything?"

"I'll be fine." *I would like an alternate universe, please.* "I love you, too. Thanks for calling."

"No problem. Oh, and Jane, do you think you will be in tomorrow? Dick is kind of fa-lipping that you aren't here right before the art fair."

Dick Reese is my boss, and I am quite certain, the minion of the Antichrist. That same flower that Victor could inspire to bloom? One sidelong glance from Dick and it would shrivel and instantly die. The Fall Art Fair begins in two weeks. Two weeks isn't "right before." And anyway, all that's left to be done is order the Reese's peanut butter cups we give away. Dick loves preening in our booth, smiling his reptilian smile when people compliment him on how clever it is that he, Dick *Reese,* has a bowl of *Reese's* peanut butter cups.

Too bad Dick is gay—I know a girl named Daisy he just might hit it off with.

"Tell Dick I will make every effort to be in tomorrow. It all depends on my back." *And it all really depends on my broken heart.* "Victor? Don't tell him my back doesn't really hurt," I added, even though I was sure he never would. I got into bed and lit a cigarette.

Ring. *No!* "Hello."

"They like artichokes!"

Oh, no. "Hi, Mom."

"Hello, dear! Elijah, Isabella, and Fideleis all love arti-chokes!" exclaimed my mother.

Elijah Darjeeling, Isabella Montgomery, and Fideleis Mc-Sween are their full names. *They* being the Schnauzers, or my siblings, depending on whom you ask. Some mothers turn their children's bedrooms into home offices or gyms when their children leave for college; some mothers leave the rooms as they are. *My* mother turned my room into a kennel; *my* mother embarked on a midlife career as a breeder of minia-ture Schnauzers.

"Really?" I said, because if I have learned anything, ever, I have learned that when it comes to my mother and it comes to the Schnauzers, there really isn't anything else to say.

"Yes! I showed Isabella how to eat the leaves by closing my teeth and pulling the leaf out. Well, needless to say she paid very close attention and when I gave her a leaf she clamped down on it with her front teeth and held on while I pulled it through. After several leaves she had it perfect! Why are you home?"

I couldn't see that relaying the recent, tragic events right then in the wake of the Schnauzers' most recent triumph would help anything. "I think I've got a twenty-four-hour thing or something," I explained instead.

"You know, I think something is going around. Fideleis hasn't been herself for days."

I wanted to be left alone forever. I thought I should get used to it, since I clearly would spend my life that way.

When the phone rang again ten minutes later and I reluc-tantly picked it up, I wondered if somehow the Schnauzers, masters of nonverbal communication that they are, had managed to convey their preference for hollandaise sauce over the more traditional melted butter.

"What's wrong? Why do you sound so miserable?" It was Kate again.

"Nothing. Nothing is wrong except the phone has been ringing and I'm tired and I need to take a nap."

"What have you been doing all morning?"

"Lying." *Go away, Kate.*

"You mean laying."

"Kate, I am going to get up tomorrow. Really."

"Really?"

"*Really*, really," I told her.

After we hung up, I was slightly cheered by the fact that *Bottle Rocket* was on cable and I could see Owen Wilson. I am desperately in love with Owen Wilson. Although I have seen *Bottle Rocket* a million times, I decided that watching it again was productive. Technically I was doing something to make myself happy. In a burst of positive feeling, I realized that while I love Owen Wilson, I have thus far been able to live without him. If I could do so well without Owen, then maybe I could find a way to live without Jack.

Maybe not.

As I went to sleep that night, every part of me dreaded how bad it would feel to wake up. I set my alarm and tried not to think about Jack Davis, whom I would never see again. I tried not to think about Dick Reese, whom, I realized, in a way that made my stomach hurt more than it had in the past two days, I would be seeing tomorrow.

3

B–R–O–W–N

"Success is a job in New York."
—Andy Warhol

I turned off Tenth Avenue, Starbucks in hand, and saw the white door with the black lettering. *Dick Reese Gallery*. I sighed. There had been a time when I thought it was such a grand entrance and such an amazing gallery. But after four years of working for Dick, of being glared at by Dick, of being corrected and demoralized by Dick, well, that feeling was long gone. I trudged for the entrance just as Victor was arriving.

"Oh. Janie. Tragique." He looked at me sadly.

"That bad?" I asked, even though I didn't want to know.

"No. You are gorgeous."

Victor took my hand and we walked through the big white door and into the reception area of the gallery. Clarissa, the receptionist, greeted us. Always very cheerful, very high-strung, and very hardworking, Clarissa is also slightly bizarre. She has a remarkably loud phone voice, and has been at the gallery since I started as an assistant. When I got promoted to manager (which is really just like an assistant, but still) she never asked for more responsibility and never tried to better her own position. She was afraid that if she did, Dick would fire her.

Actually, we are *all* afraid that Dick will one day fire us. Every six months or so, someone will get called into his office, his door will shut, and ten minutes later they leave crying. Shortly thereafter, someone new is hired and it's like the person who went into Dick's office and had the door shut behind them never existed.

My desk is off to the side of the reception area in one of the main gallery rooms. Dick told me it was preferable to sit there because of the exposure it would give me to clients. I never quite understood what he meant by that, because if clients want help with something, I am under strict orders to call Dick immediately, and he will be the one to help them. But still, it was wonderful to know when I was promoted that I would no longer be sitting at the desk up on the second floor right outside his office, getting up every time Dick yelled, "JANE!"

Victor gave me a quick reassuring hug and walked upstairs. I went to my desk and sat thinking about how much e-mail I would have. With Dick being insane, phone conversations at work are out, so I love e-mail. As I clicked on the little envelope icon, Dick slithered into view.

For a short, fat little man, he manages to move quite stealthily.

"Hi, Dick." I tried to sound cheerful and reverential, yet like someone who had genuinely been home with a hurt back. As he very often did, he narrowed his eyes at me, scowled, then turned around and walked away. Before I could get back to my e-mail, my intercom beeped. At the Dick Reese Gallery, we must answer our intercoms by saying our names, as if we are picking up an outside call. This is because Dick frequently hits the wrong numbers on his phone. This way, when he connects to the wrong person he knows right away and can hang up on them rather than being burdened by saying, "Sorry, I dialed you by mistake."

"Jane Laine." My mother named her dogs Isabella Darjeeling, Elijah Montgomery, and Fideleis McSween. Two names each; seven, seven, and five syllables respectively. Given that their last name, Laine, is so short, concise, *ordinary*, she wanted them to have special, unique-sounding names. I don't think it occurs to her that dogs don't really have last names. I don't think it occurs to her that my name is *Jane*.

"Jane." It was Dick. "Ian has just finished a magnificent piece, *Untitled: Black and Silver*. Sarah Claymoore is writing about it for *Art News*. I want you to be sure she has everything she needs in terms of visuals and biographical information on the artist."

"Sure, Dick. I'll get that done right now."

"Yes, you will. I also want an offering letter on the piece to go out to Peter Br—"

Dick's intercom has been broken for two months. It will just cut out at random, inopportune times such as this one, causing whomever he is on the phone with to miss out on valuable pieces of information. I had explained this to him, and had also tried to switch his phone one day, but he told me that I needed to get out of his office.

"I'm sorry—Peter who?" I listened to Dick exhale very loudly.

"B-r-o—" The intercom cut out again.

"Hold on, Dick. I'm coming upstairs." As I hung up, I wondered if I should explain to him, again, about the intercom being broken. I walked up the stairs and Amanda, his newest assistant, turned to look at me. She reminded me startlingly of a Velociraptor from *Jurassic Park*. Her eyes were very wide and as she craned her long neck, I had the unsettling feeling that she might suddenly leap from behind her desk and chase after me.

Dick's office occupies half of the second floor and is very sparse and very dark. I walked in, and there he sat—a little man behind a big desk—sneering up at me. For one wild moment I thought about telling him how awful he was. I wanted him to know that the only reason *anyone* worked for him was because he represents the most important artist of all time. And the only reason anyone stayed working for him was the fact that once you worked for Dick Reese, no other gallery would hire you. They knew he would wield his vast power to blackball any gallery that poached his staff. I also wanted to tell him he should never wear bright colors because it only drew attention to the fact that he was square-shaped.

Instead I said, "Hi. Sorry, but I couldn't hear that name."

"It is Brown," he hissed.

"Thanks."

Then he kept talking. "B. R. O.—"

"Dick. Thanks, I know how to spell *Brown*. I just couldn't hear you through the broken intercom."

He looked at me for a very long time, looked down at the pad on his desk, then looked back up at me. "B. R. O. W. N." After every letter he exhaled, as if he were either very tired or in a tremendous amount of pain.

I turned to leave.

"Jane. Stay. I am not done."

I reminded myself how hard it would be to get a job at another gallery.

"A beach dress is not appropriate for the gallery. I want you to sit in the packing room today."

I looked down at my dress. It had diagonal stripes in different pastel colors. Maybe not entirely work appropriate, but it was so hot outside I was sure an exception should be made.

"Ask Amanda to be downstairs greeting clients," he continued, not missing a beat. "Also, ask Amanda to send the letter on Ian's new work to Peter Brown. I want *you* to focus *completely* on getting everything ready for the art fair. You do remember that we will have only Ian Rhys-Fitzsimmons' artwork in the booth? Call Ian and get a list of what he wants to exhibit."

Ian Rhys-Fitzsimmons. An abstract sculptor originally from London, and without question the most important artist in New York or anywhere else. Years from now, chapters in art history textbooks will undoubtedly be titled *Early Twenty-First-Century Sculpture: Ian Rhys-Fitzsimmons*. Really. He is that important. Around the mid-1990s, when art critics and curators began talking in earnest about the "death of painting," Ian burst onto the scene with sculptures that, in many ways, looked like three-dimensional paintings. His work was larger than life and the art world loved it. Suddenly it was impossible to open up a copy of *Art News* or *Art Forum* or even the Arts and Leisure section of *The New York Times* without seeing some reference to Ian and his work.

That being said, I am ashamed to admit that I don't understand it.

Even though I have a master's degree in art history, I could never explain Ian's work to someone, or pinpoint what is so "it" about his sculptures. I used to think I was very good at explaining what was so "it" about Contemporary artists and their work. I used to give tours at the Whitney Museum, I wrote my thesis on Andy Warhol, and really, I got it. I used to be able to speak knowledgeably and confidently about Warhol's painting of common objects, his use of images from popular culture, his search for freshness in art. But the words that stand out now are *used to*. I used to have a clue, I used to know what was going on. But that was before. Long before Ian, and long before Dick. Now sometimes I am pretty sure the only thing I know is nothing.

And frankly, I really don't like Ian.

Before I worked for Dick, I thought it would be so exciting, so truly inspirational to be in the same place as such an artistic genius. But really, it isn't inspiring or awesome at all. It is stressful. Whenever anything to do with Ian comes up,

Dick becomes more insecure, vile, hostile, condescending, petty, and just purely evil than usual. Ian's mere presence makes my life at the Dick Reese Gallery that much more difficult. I try to avoid contact with him at all costs.

For Dick, it's just the opposite. Being Ian's dealer has made him tremendously powerful. And Dick knows that the bulk of his power is tied up in Ian, so he makes every fawning effort to keep his star happy. He knows better than anyone that the departure of Ian Rhys-Fitzsimmons would instantaneously plummet the status of the Dick Reese Gallery from "The Best Gallery in New York" to simply "a gallery in New York."

I tried to shrug off all negative thoughts as I walked down the hall past *Untitled #9*, a large pastel-green sculpture of Ian's, and headed toward the back offices. I took a seat next to our art handler, Sam, who always seems to be on drugs. I tried to focus on the task at hand—preparing for the Fall Art Fair.

I'd already ordered paint for the walls of our booth, arranged art transport for installation day, and sent out free tickets. These went to clients who will spend $600,000 on a sculpture without a second thought, but who become angry and insulted if asked to spend $5 for an admission ticket. I also printed up copies of Ian's bios and put aside two boxes of his most recent catalogues. I had written a press release that Amanda then rewrote, because Dick felt I wasn't properly "capturing the artist's importance." I could type up a price list of the works in the show, but that wouldn't be possible until Ian decided what pieces he wanted to include.

Maybe I should call him? No, no, I really didn't want to talk to Ian. Not today. How had I actually thought coming in to work would be better than staying at home? Coming to work only served to remind me that I despised my boss, that I didn't understand the greatest artistic genius of our time, and that the thing I had liked best about my life was Jack.

I'd send Ian an e-mail.

At five-thirty, the gallery closed to the public. I checked with Clarissa to see if there were any late clients scheduled to come in. There weren't, so I interrupted Sam the art handler's fifty-seventh game of Freecell, to tell him I was going back out front. "Dude," was his response; why, I am not sure.

Returning to my desk I sent the e-mail to Ian, asking for his final list of works to be included at the fair. Then I finally checked my e-mails from the past two days. None of them were exciting. Just the usual CNN Breaking News and Daily Candy and an e-mail that told me I could "Earn $1,000 A Day at Home!!" That would be nice. Jcrew.com was having a sale, but when weren't they? There was one from Kate checking in, and one from Elizabeth inviting me to a wine tasting next week. I sat there deleting messages and then it hit me.

I had forgotten to call the candy wholesalers.

Thank God I remembered!

Forgetting the Reese's peanut butter cups would be equal to forgetting to send every last one of the Rhys-Fitzsimmons sculptures to the fair. How could I have almost forgotten them? I dialed the number of the wholesale candy distributor we always use. I prayed Dick wouldn't walk downstairs at that very moment and know that I was so late in placing the order. A man with an accent answered, said, "Yes," and hung up on me. Twice. I dialed a third time. The same man answered.

"Eh-lo," he said.

"Hello! This is Jane at Dick Reese Gallery. I would like to order twenty boxes of Reese's peanut butter cups, please. Individually wrapped."

There was silence. Then he coughed. "Many?" he said.

I could sense I was losing him. "Yes, yes. TWENTY boxes. Can they be delivered by TOMORROW at three-thirty?"

"Is one-fifty." He hung up.

It was okay. If they didn't arrive tomorrow, I still had plenty of time to call again. The fair opened in exactly two weeks. The candy would be staying in the packing room until then anyway. I was totally on top of this. I e-mailed Dick because I didn't want to talk to him, and imagined him being pleased that I had both remembered and taken care of every last detail. I was a go-getter.

Mail to: Dick@DickReeseGallery.com

From: Jane@DickReeseGallery.com

Re: Reese's Peanut Butter Cups for the Fall Art Fair

DR: The peanut butter cups for the Fall Art Fair will be delivered tomorrow by 3:30. Can you please write a check for $150.00? Thanks, Jane

His answer came back swiftly.

Mail to: Jane@DickReeseGallery.com

From: Dick@DickReeseGallery.com

Re: Re: Reese's Peanut Butter Cups for the Fall Art Fair

I cannot very well write a check to no one. I do not know if you know this. Apparently you do not. Then anyone could cash it. You need to not feed me information piecemeal. It is not possible for me to relate to that efficiently. To whom do I write the check?

Why? Why? Why? Fuck. Fuck. Fuck.

Mail to: Dick@DickReeseGallery.com
From: Jane@DickReeseGallery.com
Re: Re: Re: Reese's Peanut Butter Cups for the Fall Art Fair
Happy Wholesalers.

Dick has been obsessed with ordering Reese's peanut butter cups since time began. One would *think* he would know the name of the wholesaler. Especially since he wrote a check to them *every year.* I wondered, not for the first time, *If I am continually treated as the stupidest person in the world, will I slowly become her?* Defeated and sulky, I waited for Dick to come downstairs and leave. When he finally appeared, he silently put a check on my desk and then went to the closet to get his cape.

"Iiiii am off to see Hup Jump A La Ya," he singsonged, apparently no longer in a snit over the piecemeal information.

"That sounds like a lovely evening. Have a nice time." *I hate you.*

"Are you familiar with Hup Jump A La Ya?" He looked down at me.

"Um . . ." *Why couldn't I have just said good-bye?* Dick lived to make anyone under forty-five or straight know they were a cultural wasteland. I had absolutely no idea what it was. It could be a movie? Maybe a band? A troupe of inner-city youths armed only with their love for the spoken word? "No."

He exhaled, as though to teach me anything would take him a million lifetimes. "Good night, Jane."

As soon as the door slammed shut behind him I went to Google and searched for the phrase "Hup Jump A La Ya." There were no matches.

I looked one more time at my e-mail, before logging off. I was not prepared for what I found. In bold letters in my in-box, I saw **Davis, Jack.** My hands began shaking and my throat was suddenly dry. I tried to breathe a deep, cleansing breath like they teach in yoga, but it came out ragged, as if I was dying. I double-clicked on his name.

Mail to: Jane@DickReeseGallery.com

Mail from: Davisjack99@hotmail.com

Jane, I need to say for the record that I don't appreciate the violation of privacy of your being in my apartment without my permission.

That said, I am sorry for the way you found things out. It was never my intention to hurt you. I just want to be happy, Jane, and I wasn't. I decided to move on and it is a healthy thing. I hope that you will be able to do the same. I know this is probably very hard on you right now but I believe that you will be a better person and a stronger person for going through this. I think I am. Please take care.

Best, Jack

I deleted the message, and then double-deleted it from the trash folder. Otherwise I would have tortured myself for days reading it over and over again. *When has Jack ever cared about health,* I wondered bitterly, *emotional or otherwise?* Why did he think I needed to be a better and stronger person? How, in any way, could he think I was going to *benefit* from any of this? He said it all as if he hadn't broken my heart, but rather as if he had done some really nice favor for me!

And had he *actually said* he thought he was now a *better person?*

I needed to read the e-mail again, but it was gone.

Up to that point a part of me had been holding a vigil for Jack. I could see her—a miniature version of myself, sitting inside my head, in a miniature version of Central Park. She was sitting on a bench, completely alone, holding a candle, waiting patiently for all of the dreams about a future with Jack to come true. As I shut down my computer and left the gallery that night, the miniature person inside me finally stood up from that bench and blew out her candle.

4

BREAKUP ETIQUETTE

"What makes a person spend time being sad
when they could be happy?"
—Andy Warhol

Dick goes to his house in the Pines section of Fire Island almost every weekend, so he's rarely in the gallery on Fridays. As a result, Fridays are the least stressful days of the week. This particular Friday, I got an e-mail from Ian, with the list of what he wanted exhibited at the fair. He followed up with a call, and was actually very agreeable; all the pieces he wanted were ones that were either at the gallery or in his nearby studio. Clarissa and I worked together on the price list and exhibition labels and before I knew it, it was the end of the day.

· · ·

On Saturday, I slept late, took two naps, and then organized my closet.

I pulled out anything that belonged to Jack (two suits, a couple of pairs of khakis, some shirts, a pair of jeans, a baseball cap, five ties, and a pair of sneakers) and shoved it into a garbage bag. I thought I would give everything to Goodwill or the Salvation Army. Then I thought I should return his things, stoically and gracefully, saying we simply weren't meant to be. I passed on that impulse and dragged the bag down the hall and threw it into the garbage chute.

On Sunday, I decided I would go to see my parents, who live an hour away from the city. I dialed home and my mom answered. Actually, it could have been anyone that answered—it was so hard to tell with all the Schnauzers clamoring in the background.

"Hi, Mom, it's Jane," I yelled.

"Hello, darling. Isabella! Elijah! Fideleis! Please! Yes, darling, how are you today?"

"Mom. Jack and I broke up."

"Oh dear. Isabella, if I have told you once I have told you a thousand times that is NOT a chew toy! This is sudden? Whatever happened? Are you okay? Elijah Darjeeling, sweet pea, please, please at least contemplate joining us for breakfast."

Elijah has an eating disorder and will eat only occasionally, and then, only if coaxed.

"No! No! No! Fideleis, no! Jane. I am so sorry. What can we do? FIDELEIS! NO!"

I hadn't been able to tell her about it before, not when the Schnauzers were eating artichokes and all, but right then I wanted so much to tell her about the daisies. I wanted to hear that everything was going to be okay; that life would go on as it always did and that soon enough this would all be a distant memory. I did not want to hear that Fideleis needed to stop tormenting Elijah. I did not want to hear that Isabella shouldn't chew on the phone cord. "Mom. I thought I would come out for the day."

"Oh, sweetheart. I wish you had told us earlier. I am so sorry, but your father and I aren't going to be here today."

"Why?" I asked but I already knew the answer.

"Fideleis, don't start. Darling, Dad and I are going to drive out to Sag Harbor with Isabella. She has family there."

In order to reconcile what she sees as the cruelty of separating puppies from their mothers, Mom keeps tabs on the locations of any and all pups she has sold. She and my father will take road trips with either Isabella, Elijah, or Fideleis for a visit with their long-lost offspring. Sometimes it's only a few hours' drive. Sometimes it is much farther. One year we all went to Aspen for Thanksgiving to celebrate with a descendant of Isabella. Elijah and Fideleis came, too, even though it wasn't technically their family we were visiting.

"Fine. I'll call you during the week," I snapped, hating the Schnauzers and hating the world.

"Jane, do I hear a tone?"

"No, Mom. There isn't a tone. Call me when you get back. Say hi to Dad for me."

"Okay, dear. You feel better. Maybe go to a museum or something to get your mind off things. Have you been to the Met recently?"

I said good-bye quickly and hung up the phone. I called

Kate and we talked for a little while, and then I called Elizabeth and we made plans to go to a wine tasting with her fiancé, Craig.

And that was that. The weekend was over.

The wine tasting was held on Tuesday night, at this very talked-about new wine store downtown called Grape. It was ultra-hip and cool inside and had been written up in all the magazines and on all the New York City Web sites. When I arrived, Elizabeth was waiting right near the door for me, which was nice of her but made me wonder if she thought I would burst into flames at the prospect of having to arrive at a party by myself. Everywhere I looked I saw stainless steel and perfectly organized bottles of wine. There were also several dashing men who appeared to work there, telling people what was what. It was all image and packaging, but it was worlds more fun than the liquor store on my corner. Elizabeth immediately began steering me toward Craig in the back of the shop. As we reached him, I realized in despair why she was being so insistent.

"Jane! Hi!" Craig said with a fake smile. "This is a great buddy of mine from my law school days, Greg Jensen. Greg, this is Elizabeth's friend, Jane Laine. Jane works at Dick Reese Gallery."

No! No, no, no. Not a setup! Elizabeth chose to ignore the death rays I was shooting at her, and as she smiled a really enthusiastic, thumbs-up sort of smile, she, along with Craig, disappeared.

"So. Dick Reese Gallery. Never heard of it. What sort of stuff do you do there?"

I knew I shouldn't judge him right away. "Contemporary art. Sculpture mostly." I had to be polite, but except for being tall, there wasn't anything appealing about him. "What do you do?"

"Lawyer," he said as he looked over my head and scanned the room behind me.

I realized it was my turn to say something, but what? "Lawyering, I hear that's nice"? *Where.* That's it! "Where?"

"What?"

His cell phone started to ring and he picked it up and began a conversation with someone named Old Boy. He continued talking and it didn't seem like he was going to finish anytime soon. I could go to the bathroom. Then would I have to come back? Someone handed me a glass of wine. I looked up, expecting to see Elizabeth and prepared to shun her, but instead I saw that the glass of wine was being handed to me by one of the dashing-looking wine store men.

"Cell phones really are the death of manners, aren't they?"

On closer inspection, dashing man actually wasn't as dashing as his suit—but he had given me wine and saved me from standing by myself in the middle of the party.

"Mitch Henderson." He extended his hand and smiled.

I shook his hand and told him my name and for a minute forgot about everything that had happened in the last week. It turned out Mitch knew Greg Jensen, so the three of us talked and Greg didn't seem so miserable. Several glasses of wine later, it wasn't such a bad evening and I wasn't even that mad at Elizabeth when she reappeared to tell me she and Craig were headed home and asked did I want to stay. I've never been very good at leaving a party while I'm still having fun, and I thought this might be a good time to start, so I said good night to Greg and Mitch and joined Elizabeth at the door.

"Didn't you like Greg?" she asked.

"He was fine," I told her. "It's you I don't like very much right now."

"I thought it would be fun—" she began.

"I don't want to date anyone right now." As soon as I said it, I felt a tap on my shoulder. I turned around and it was Mitch. Either he hadn't heard me, or he liked a challenge. He asked me if I was free the next Wednesday.

"I am," I told him and ignored Elizabeth's staged try at keeping a straight face.

"Great," he said and wrote down my number.

5

PINOT NOIR

"When you're interested in somebody
and you think they might be interested
in you, you should point out all your beauty
problems and defects right away, rather than
take a chance they won't notice them."
—Andy Warhol

Mitch Henderson, dashing wine guy, called me the next day to say he had enjoyed meeting me and asked if I would like to go to Central Park with him for a picnic and a performance of the Philharmonic the following Wednesday. *What a lovely idea,* I thought. We talked for a little bit, and he said he would take care of bringing the food and wine. I asked if I could bring anything, and he suggested I bring a blanket and some wine glasses. *Easy enough.*

"So, let's just meet on the steps of the Met at seven?"

"Okay. See you there," I said.

Willing Dick to stay upstairs, I looked to make sure there weren't any clients around. If I'd already risked one call, why not two? I dialed Kate to fill her in.

"I have a good feeling about this," she told me. "Maybe he will come for dinner in Miami one day!"

Kate and I have a long-standing belief that as soon as I find "the one," the man who will make all of my dreams come true, I will invite him to dinner at her house in Miami. Jack didn't like Miami and never wanted to spend any of his vacation time there, so I had never been able to invite him to dinner at Kate's. Kate says that was a definite, unmistakable sign that he and I were never meant to be.

The following Wednesday at the gallery was uneventful. Unfortunately, by the time it was five-thirty and I was ready to go, Dick still hadn't appeared to say something obnoxious to me, don his summer cape, and leave. There isn't any rule stating that gallery workers have to stay until he leaves. We just do. No one wants to be the person whom Dick can't find when he is having a meltdown. Sitting at your desk doing nothing until dawn is preferable to what you would have to endure if you weren't around when Dick was having an art emergency.

I decided to chance it.

I turned off my computer and started toward home, figuring I would have just enough time to spruce up, pack a blanket, and get to the Met by seven. I was feeling surprisingly happy as I headed into the subway wondering, *Should I bring the light blue blanket or the green one?*

You only get a nice, new train when you aren't in a rush and it isn't hot.

I was stuffed into the oldest relic still running, and we got held on the tracks for twenty minutes. I began to wonder if we would stay there forever, and I would be forced to become friends with all the miserable, angry people who were more or less stepping on my head. By the time I got home I was sweaty and gross and it was six-thirty. I didn't want to be late so I didn't change; I was wearing a blue skirt, one of my favorites and definitely good for a date. I fixed my makeup, brushed my hair, grabbed the light blue blanket and two wine glasses, stuffed them into a canvas boat bag I found in the closet, and ran out the door. There was just enough time to get over to the Met.

I walked to Fifth Avenue and then walked up to the museum. I noticed that the light blue of my blanket matched exactly the light blue of the handles on the boat bag. I wondered if that made me look like a dork. I looked at the light blue color of my skirt and answered my own question.

I got to the steps of the Met at exactly seven o'clock.

I sat down at the north end near the entrance to the park, put the light blue bag and blanket disaster behind me, and checked my lipstick. I set about arranging myself in a generally fetching manner when my cell phone started to ring. I didn't want to be talking on the phone when Mitch arrived so I thought about not answering. Then I thought it could *be* Mitch. I put the phone to my ear.

"Hello?"

"Jane. Hi. It's Mitch. I'm going to be about five minutes late."

"Okay." He could say, "I'm sorry," I thought. But all he said was "Bye," and hung up before I could say anything else. It was okay though; it was only five minutes after seven, and five minutes isn't such a big deal. So I returned to making myself look fetching.

At seven-thirty, I was annoyed.

At seven-forty, I decided it would be better to leave rather than be the big loser who waits around, sitting on a street corner, for a date. I turned to pick up my bag and thought I would go to a bar alone and feel *really*, really sorry for myself. When I turned back, Mitch was standing in front of me. He leaned over and kissed me on the cheek.

"That was ridiculous."

That was all he said. He didn't say, "That was ridiculous that I was so late," or, "That was ridiculous that I was trapped under heavy furniture for thirty minutes," or, "That was ridiculous that my cell phone worked once to call you but then didn't work to call you a second time."

"What was ridiculous?" I asked. "How late you were?"

He said, "Ha-ha," but I wasn't trying to be funny. I really wanted to know.

He rolled his eyes at me in an "oh-you-are-a-spoiled-and-high-maintenance-sort-of-girl" type of way and asked if I was ready to go. I said yes, and he started walking toward the park without offering to carry the boat bag. I walked quickly next to him in order to keep up. He wasn't making any attempt at conversation so I went back to my original question.

"So, did you get caught up at work?"

"Fires at the office. Fires that I needed to put out. One of my co-workers was really upset so I had to smooth things over by taking him for a drink."

Okay, so basically he was out having a drink with a work buddy. And also he was so, so very important that the only way a fire could be put out at his "office" was if he, and he alone, intervened and smoothed things out?

"Business. Politics. Pressure. You know how it is," Mitch explained.

I didn't. The bulk of the boat bag kept banging into my leg.

"Crazy. Hectic time," he added.

All I could think was, *He works in a wine store!*

We were so late getting into the park, and so many people had come to listen to the symphony, that finding a place near the stage was definitely not an option. Finding a place far away from the stage was even proving to be quite difficult. We settled on some rather sad real estate near a cement path and some Porto-Sanis. I wasn't sure if the Philharmonic had started yet, or if we were simply too far away to hear it. I unfolded the blanket and saw his eyes flick from blue to blue to blue. Then he went about opening his very small and, I am sure not very heavy, bag, removing two bottles of wine and a wedge of Brie.

"Oh. That's what I forgot. Bread. It's always something, isn't it?" he said and threw me what I guess he thought was a winning, boyish smile.

Yeah, it is, I thought. *It is always something.* Even though Cupid was blatantly sleeping on the job, at least my friend

Bacchus was watching over me; Mitch was already busying himself opening what he was telling me was a really "special" bottle of red zinfandel. It was very "exciting," he told me.

"Thanks," I said after he poured some into my glass. I finished mine while Mitch was still swirling his around, sniffing and reswirling.

As we finished the bottle, or rather as I finished three and a half glasses and he swished his around looking out at me from under heavy-lidded eyes, I didn't feel so bad anymore. The more I drank, the more I thought he was really sort of cute. *Yes, definitely*, I thought, *I am having a nice time.* Not having any bread or a knife made it difficult to eat the Brie unless one of us were to pick it up like a slice of pizza. I decided against that and ignored how hungry I felt. I drank some more.

Suddenly our location near the potties didn't seem so bad.

I told Mitch I would be right back, then had to walk a bit farther than I had planned because of a very long line. "Jane! Jane Laine? Hey! Is that you?" I heard as I walked past a blanket with plates and different types of cheeses, several baguettes, crackers and fruit and salamis and ham. *Look at all the different hams and salamis. Oh, I love the lami!* Who were these beautiful creatures and how did I know them? I dragged my attention away from the food and realized who it was—Craig's friend from law school, with a couple I didn't know.

"Jane! Greg Jensen. We met the other night at the wine tasting. What are you doing here?" he asked.

"Greg, hi. I'm actually here with Mitch Henderson. How are you?"

"Fine, fine. Where are you sitting?"

"Oh, just over there." I turned around to point, hoping we would be invited to join them and have some of their food.

"Why don't you join us?"

Bingo. When I got back to my blanket, Mitch was heavily into a conversation on his cell phone. What about cell phones being the death of manners? After he hung up, I told him about Greg and the other couple and how they invited us to join them. He agreeably got up and we walked back to their blanket.

The other two people were named Cindy and Matthew. They gave me a glass of wine and told Mitch and me they hoped we hadn't eaten. Oh, they were lovely people, they were. I happily ate Brie on crackers and salami on baguette and drank a wine that wasn't described to me, until I remembered I still had to go to the bathroom. I left Mitch chatting with Greg and went off again to the Porto-Sani line.

I was standing in line and every now and then the symphony would hit a crescendo I could hear and that was nice. Then things around me started to spin just the slightest, tiniest bit. I watched four people heading off toward the trees, presumably because the bathroom line was so long. I wanted to run across the lawn to the tree people yelling, "Take me! Take me with you!" But then, soon enough, it was my turn.

I walked back to the blanket where Mitch and Greg and the lovely couple were. Mitch didn't seem to be chatting anymore with Greg and was sitting there in what looked very much like a snit. I weighed the pros and cons of having some sliced melon over going back to our original spot. I asked

Mitch if he wanted to go back to our blanket. He said quickly that he did, and we got up and said our good-byes. On the way back I asked if anything was wrong.

"If you wanted to spend a night with your friends you should have done that."

Was he serious? Wasn't Greg his friend? He wasn't mine; I just met him, and what did it matter anyway? Walking to the blanket in silence, I felt like I was having a fight with my boyfriend, except with Jack, we never once had such a stupid, petty disagreement. When we got back I thought about just folding the blanket up—then Mitch sat down on it. After a few moments he leaned toward me very quickly and kissed me. I thought, *I hate this guy.* But even though he was late, rolled his eyes at me, didn't offer to carry my bag, and got into a snit for no reason, I kissed him back. The last person I had kissed, the only person I had kissed for years, had been Jack. I thought maybe kissing someone else would make it easier to forget him, not think about him five times every minute. As Mitch pulled me down onto the blanket, somewhere in the background I heard, "Get a room."

It hit me then how drunk I was.

I was lying in front of a huge crowd of people on line for the toilet, making out with a stranger. I pulled away and said, "Really, we shouldn't."

"Fine then, let's leave."

Mitch got up quickly, right back in his snit. I started to fold the blanket as the smell of smoke wafted past me. One of the nearby people, a blond guy in a striped oxford shirt, was smoking a cigarette. I thought, *Damn it all to hell,* and asked him if I could have one. He offered the pack, and as

I took one I noticed he had really pretty green eyes. I felt ashamed for being white trash and making out three feet away from him.

"Are you ready?" Mitch said as he started walking quickly out of the park.

"Could you carry the bag for me?" I asked as nicely as I could, given the circumstances. I didn't want to let it lie. I couldn't believe anyone could be this much of an idiot.

"It's your bag. Not mine," he snapped.

As soon as we got out of the park he asked me, "How far away do you live?"

Did he think he was coming home with me? Could he really? Even one block would be way too much farther to walk with Mitch. He stood there waiting for me to answer him and I thought he looked a little like Dick might, were he to lose forty pounds. "Mitch, thanks for the wine. I'm all set."

I put my arm up. A taxi stopped right away and I got in quickly. As I rode down Fifth Avenue, I closed my eyes so I wouldn't have to see all the people leaving the park and holding hands on the sidewalk.

6

REESE'S PIECES

"Art is what you can get away with."
—Andy Warhol

Thursday night was the gala opening of the Fall Art Fair and Thursday afternoon was the special preview for the press, so that morning everything was as busy as could be at the Dick Reese Gallery. This was a blessing because the busier I was, the less time I had to think about the date with Mitch, my tremendous wine hangover, and the fact that I was trailer park trash and was going to be alone forever.

As the morning sped along, I noticed with satisfaction that everything seemed to be going perfectly. The fair was being held at the Sixty-seventh Street Armory; Dick had been there since very early in the morning. He wanted to be sure he was there the first time Ian came to the booth. It was nice to be at the gallery without him. Without his endless intercomming, I had time to think about the opening party, where the most impressive sales are made. All the sculptures would sell and my tireless attention to detail, organizing every last aspect of the fair, would be rewarded. Maybe I would be given a modicum of respect?

"DICK REESE GALLERY!" Clarissa picked up another call.

My intercom beeped. "Jane Laine," I said out of sheer habit, even though I could see Clarissa intercomming me.

"DICK! LINE 5!"

"Thanks, Clarissa." Could Dick be calling to praise me already? "Hi Di—"

"Openendthrrrboxessssreesespeanutrrrandtheynotmin-igrrgaaaharethebiggrgrgg!"

He was speaking very, very quickly in a high-pitched voice. While he was not nearly as loud as Clarissa, his volume was high.

"Openendthrrrboxessssreesespeanutrrrandtheynotmin-igrrgaaaharethebiggrgrgg!"

"I'm sorry?" I had no idea what he was saying, but I had a clear idea it wasn't good. My thoughts of praise ran around in a frenzy, grabbing their bags and getting the hell out of Dodge.

"Youyoushouldbesorryyoushouldbesorryeverythingisru-inedjustrruinedIjustopenedtheboxesofreesespeanutbutter cupsgleprrtheyhsrguparenotminiblehbleyarethebigones!"

Okay. "I should be sorry" was said twice. *Okay, okay.* "Everything is just ruined," did I hear that? Dick slowed down a bit, and with horror, I could finally understand what he was saying.

"They! Are! Not! Mini!"

They are not mini. Sweat was forming rapidly on my palms and behind my knees and on the back of my neck. What he had been screeching was, "I just opened the boxes of Reese's peanut butter cups and they are not mini!" *I ordered regular-sized Reese's peanut butter cups?* This was very, very, very bad. It was a mistake that had never been made, not since Dick had first become obsessed with the candy, which was when time began. My career was over. My name was mud. I was never, ever going to work in the art world again.

"I am so sorry. I—I don't know what went wrong. I'll call the wholesaler and exchange them!" My face was turning red from the sweltering heat. Why had the temperature of the gallery changed so dramatically? I pulled a piece of tape off the roll on my desk and rolled it into a little cigarette-like tube. I put it in my mouth and chewed on it.

"No. We have already paid for them." Ex-haaale.

"I will pay for new ones myse—" I tried, desperate.

"Do not interrupt ME. You work for ME and are not to interrupt ME," he screamed. I didn't know what to do. Should I say something or would that be interrupting? Was he finished? Was there a period or a comma after the "ME"? *Oh, God.*

"Are you there, Jane?" Still at high pitch.

"I am so sorry, Dick. I can call right now and get them exchanged."

"No, I do not want that. It is too late. Enough. We will all just have to suffer through this incompetence. Transfer me to Victor."

I didn't say good-bye or anything else; I just quickly punched the transfer button and Victor's extension and felt myself deflate. I exhaled and looked over at Clarissa, whose eyes were wide and concerned. She looked as if she was going to cry. I turned and stared at my computer screen.

Victor came down the stairs. "Dick said he was feeling faint, so I am going to get him a banana juice and run it up to the Armory. He mentioned the Reese's peanut butter cups. Rough, Janie. I know they have the mini ones at the deli. Do you want me to buy some?"

"No. He doesn't want that," I snapped.

"DICK REESE GALLERY!" Clarissa, at least, seemed to have bounced back quickly.

Sixty of the top galleries from all over the world gather at the Fall Art Fair. Each gallery has a booth about forty feet by twenty feet where they display their finest paintings, drawings, and sculptures. It is amazing to see such top-quality old masters, nineteenth-century, impressionist, modern, American, and contemporary art all under one roof. The Fall Art Fair is the first big event of the season, and the sale results set the tone for the market. If an artist's work doesn't sell well at this fair, it can tarnish the artist's or dealer's commercial value for the entire year or even longer. A tense excitement fills the air between the rows and rows of gallery booths. There are other important art fairs that take place throughout the year, such as the London Contemporary Art Fair in October and the *Arte Contemporaneo* in Rome in November. Those are smaller, but still distinctive. Then there's the

Chicago Art Fair, in December, but it's not as popular because of the cold. Not so the Art Dealers Federation Fair in Santa Fe in January and the Miami Art Fair in February. The season ends with Art Basel in June—the only fair to rival the Fall Art Fair in importance and prestige.

Our booth was in the prime location right near the entrance to the fair. The first art that any collector or member of the press would see for the season would be Dick Reese's installation of four Ian Rhys-Fitzsimmons sculptures. Everyone from the gallery was required to be in the booth for the opening night festivities. I tried to spend as much of the evening as I could in the small, five-by-five-foot closet built into the booth's corner. We keep things in there like catalogues, price lists, press packages, a mirror for Dick to gaze at himself, and tonight, the extra, hateful, regular-sized Reese's peanut butter cups. I would pretend I was going in there to get something, and would stay for as long as I thought feasible before someone noticed. Then I would come back out and Dick would glare at me.

When I wasn't in the closet, I saw that Ian, at least, seemed to be having a wonderful time. What was it like to be only thirty-five and have everyone you know, and everyone you don't, shower you constantly with praise? Ian smiled frequently and said "Thank you" quite often. It was hard to tell if he was blushing, uncomfortable from all of the praise, or if he was just hot from standing underneath the spotlights. People kept taking his picture, and I wondered if he had considered this before he selected the extremely loud purple plaid shirt he was wearing. Magazine writers often describe Ian, who favors bright shirts and clashing ties, Prada loafers, and black-rimmed glasses, and whose hair always sticks up at random angles, as young, hip, and nattily dressed. They think it is clever to call him *natty* since he is from London. I don't think he looks hip or natty.

I think he looks ridiculous.

I guess it is just different for the rest of the world than it is for me. When the world was presented with Ian, they saw artistic genius wrapped up in a high-end British package. They saw this fashionable, "trendy" man who had graduated from the best English boarding schools, Oxford University, and the prestigious MFA program at Yale, achieving seemingly automatic gallery representation in New York followed by a long series of sold-out shows and press coverage and parties in his honor. He had the right artist friends and the right collector ones, too. He never got any bad press and the camera seemed to love him and he was always smiling a polite smile, always saying something that everyone said was very smart, very brilliant. That's what the rest of the world saw.

But all I ever saw was art I didn't get and a reason for my psychotic boss to become that much more insane. Sure, I can see Ian's sculptures are pretty, and fine, I can understand that they can actually make you feel happy just by looking at them. But beyond that—nothing. I know there has to be something more. Picasso, Matisse, Monet, there is *always* something. *Cubism, Fauvism, Impressionism.* Something you can put your finger on and read out loud. With Ian's work, I never feel that. I never feel that dash, that spark of understanding. As much as it makes me feel dumb, it also makes me wonder if maybe Ian is just a big fraud.

"Yes, thank you, indeed. It *is* about the way objects fit together. I've always been very interested in that," I could hear Ian explaining to one of the gallery's top clients. *Blah, blah, blah, Ian.* The flashing from the cameras was making me dizzy. As I walked back to the closet, out of the corner of my eye, I saw Dick smiling at Ian, raising his glass of champagne in a silent, adoring salute.

I shut the door behind me and leaned against it, standing as far away from the refill bag of peanut butter cups as possible. I thought about Ian's quiet manner, his seriousness, and his daring fashion choices. When I first met him, he'd been wearing bright orange pants and I'd thought that he was gay. Victor told me that he wasn't, he was just British.

I closed my eyes in the darkness of the closet, willing the party to end. Outside, I could hear the voice of George Oreganato, a salesperson of a nearby gallery, asking for me. I opened the door and saw he'd already moved on. I went back into the booth, and stood with my arms crossed so I would look unapproachable and no one would talk to me or ask me to explain Ian's work. I stared into the aisle and listened to Dick describe what a truly remarkable contribution *Untitled: Red and Blue* was to contemporary art. I stared harder until everything lost focus and wondered if what everyone was saying was true. Just because bunches of people say something is good, is it? *How much importance,* I wondered, *should anyone really place on what other people say? On what other people tell you to feel?*

My mind snapped back to the present as I overheard Alexandra Wentschmidt, the dealer whose booth was next to ours, asking Dick why, this year, he had regular-sized Reese's peanut butter cups when every other year, for as long as she could remember, he'd had mini-sized. I didn't turn around but could feel Dick's beady, soulless eyes burning into my back.

"It was the oversight of a careless staff member," he said and I was sure that he was rolling his eyes. "It really is terrible."

"You must be devastated!" she exclaimed. It was as if he had paid this woman to act out some demented drama he had scripted.

"Oh, I am," he said and then exhaled very loudly. "Truly devastated. Deeply, deeply distraught."

7

IAN RHYS-FITZSIMMONS:
THE ART FAIR PROJECT

"Making money is art and working is art and
good business is the best art of all."
—Andy Warhol

"Jane Laine."

"Jane," Dick said in the very nice voice he uses with Ian, and with people who are interested in buying Ian's work, "could you come to my office?" Then quickly he added, "Please," so it almost sounded as if it had been part of the original thought. For Dick, it was the conversational equivalent of skating a quadruple axel—very rarely attempted, and extremely difficult to execute. It was one week after the art fair, and he hadn't asked me to do a thing since, nor had he spoken to me.

Cautiously I grabbed a pen and pad and headed up the stairs.

As I walked into the vast expanse of white and chrome and shadow that is Dick's office, he stood up. He walked past me and shut the door. I heard the handle click and I knew then what was about to happen. I looked down at the pen and paper I had brought with me and wondered if I was the only person who had been ready to take notes at their firing. He asked me to sit and I knew I would be one of the crying people once the door opened again and I was on the other side of it.

"Jane. With the glaring exception of the Reese's peanut butter cups, which hopefully we can put behind us, I want to commend you on doing an excellent job of organizing the art fair."

"Thank you," I answered. Was this what happened when you got fired from the Dick Reese Gallery? You finally got some praise, some acknowledgment? Maybe all the crying people cried not because they were upset about being fired, but because they were so overcome that something complimentary had been said to them at last?

"The final Rhys-Fitzsimmons from the fair sold yesterday afternoon," he went on. "So that makes another sold-out fair for the gallery. And for Ian, of course."

Why is he telling me this?

"Ian's sculptures always sell well, as I think you are aware," he continued in a lecturing voice.

Yes, Dick, even I am aware of that.

"What Ian has pointed out, and the idea he and I have been toying with, is that while the sculptures always sell, they never sell as effortlessly as at the fairs. Similarly, the press is always that much more exuberant in its reaction to Ian's work when it is seen against the backdrop of an art fair. It is one of the many fascinating and intriguing aspects of Ian's work, that it becomes even stronger—even more intense and powerful in its dynamism—when seen in the context of commercialism and in the company of other art."

"Against the backdrop," "fascinating and intriguing aspects," "powerful in its dynamism." He sounds like he's reading copy from an Ian Rhys-Fitzsimmons press release. Written by Amanda.

"And of course, gallery sales of Ian's work are always much stronger *after* the New York fairs; that should be easily understandable."

Yes, Dick, it is easily understandable.

"What Ian plans to do, as a conceptual-art-slash-performance-piece-slash-commercial venture, if you will, is to go to a different art fair in a different city every month, for the next five months."

An interesting idea.

"Subsequently, after each art fair he is going to exhibit his work for the remainder of that month at given venues in whatever city he is in. He is interested in recording what sort of impact such a trip will have on the development of his oeuvre and its reception. And, of course, we are all looking forward to the sale of many artworks."

He stopped talking.

An art fair followed by a gallery exhibition in five different cities? It occurred to me that this must have been all Ian's idea in concept, and all Dick's in commercialism. It also occurred to me that this might qualify as the longest conversation Dick and I ever had. It further occurred to me that maybe I wasn't going to get fired. I looked at Dick, who seemed to be waiting for me to say something.

"That sounds like an extremely inspired idea. It should be very interesting to see the effect it has on Ian's work." I filled the silence.

"Ian wants to leave in two weeks. His plan is to go to London, Rome, Chicago, and Santa Fe; return to New York for two weeks for his retrospective that opens on the thirty-first of January; and then finish the project in Miami in February."

I thought, *What a grueling trip,* and was silently thankful I would have nothing to do with it. And maybe Dick would be nicer if Ian was away all the time? Maybe Dick would be away, too? Oh, but that would be too much to hope for.

"Will Ian be staying in hotels? Do you want me to start looking into flights for him?" I asked, guessing that was why we were having this private chat.

"No. No. Amanda has taken care of all of the flights and hotels and has been working with galleries in each of the cities. This is a tremendous undertaking, Jane," he said condescendingly. "We have been preparing for it for quite some time."

A moment ago it seemed I was the first person at the gallery to learn about the project; clearly, that was not true. Of course Dick wouldn't want me setting anything up after The Reese's Peanut Butter Cup Disaster. I could almost hear him saying how he wanted to be sure Ian was on the proper-sized plane, after all. But then why, if I wasn't to be involved at all, had he called me into his office? With his nice voice and the added "please"?

"Jane," he said, as if reading my mind, "you are going with him."

8

PLANE JANE

"I'm the type who'd be happy not going anywhere
as long as I was sure I knew exactly what was
happening at the places I wasn't going to. I'm the
type who'd like to sit home and watch every party
that I'm invited to on a monitor in my bedroom."
—Andy Warhol

I don't think it registered right away.

My brain reversed itself, skipped back in the conversation, and started over. After a brief instant replay, my mind caught up with itself. "What? Why?" I asked, wondering how long I had been staring and not saying anything. Dick didn't seem particularly annoyed, so it couldn't have been too long.

"Well, Jane." He stared at me with narrowed eyes. "For one thing, because I told you that you are."

Was he baiting me, waiting for me to say I wouldn't go? Maybe he wanted me to quit? Even though my life, at present, sucked, it sucked a lot less than living in hotels for five months with no one to talk to. I mean, what kind of conversation could I have with *Ian,* really, without feeling stupid?

"Ian needs to concentrate on his work," Dick continued. "I don't want him lifting a finger. I don't want him to carry a bag. I want the gallery to take care of that for him—I want the gallery to take care of *everything* and *you* are the representative of the gallery that I want to go."

His words flew at me like wood chips hurtling out of a tree shredder.

"Is there any way I can think about it? Or split it up with Victor or Amanda? Maybe we could each go for two months or something like that?" As the words came out of my mouth, I knew they were stupid and unprofessional.

And pointless.

I knew Dick's mind was made up and there wasn't anything that I could do.

"Jane." Dick held up his hand. "This is not up for discussion. I make the decisions here, not you. I want Amanda, Victor, Sam, and Clarissa here at the gallery with me. I want *you* to go with Ian. I want *you* to be sure everything goes smoothly for Ian. You leave in two weeks. Amanda has your plane tickets and hotel reservations. If this is something that you feel you cannot do, I will accept your resignation."

And that was that.

Dick stood up, walked to the door, and opened it. I pictured myself as a gypsy in a long, flowing skirt, carrying all of Ian's bags and whatever sculptures I could lift. I saw myself dragging a large red wagon with more sculptures crowded into it—spilling out of it—following Ian for months and months and months from art fair to art fair. I knew I wouldn't really be carrying hundred-pound sculptures, but it felt like I already was. I walked out of Dick's office praying that the Velociraptor would jump out from behind her desk. I wouldn't make her chase after me. I would just stand there and let her kill me and eat me for lunch.

I got back to my desk and saw plane tickets and an itinerary and a few thick folders marked "Art Fair Project: Art Fair Venues"; "Art Fair Project: Gallery Venues"; "Art Fair Project: Press Releases"; and "Art Fair Project: Other (by City)," sitting on my chair. I hated that Amanda put every single thing into spreadsheet format. I hate when people put things on your chair. Like you are really going to miss it if it is put on your desk? Amanda always puts things on my chair. I gathered up the folders, thinking how terribly unimportant I was in the scheme of the gallery, and how little Dick must care about my input. I hadn't been involved in the planning of any of this. He wasn't sending me because he thought I would do a great job.

He was sending me because he didn't want to part with anyone else.

Walking up Ninth Avenue, I called Kate from my cell phone.

"But you know he is so super smarty-pants. You know he is so know-it-all," I reminded her when she didn't instantly comprehend the complete atrocity of being sent away with Ian.

"Maybe he's not as bad as all that?" she tried.

Reese's peanut butter cups. Dick *Reese*. Ian *Rhys*-Fitzsimmons. *Reese* and *Rhys* swirled around in my mind and I concentrated on those two names, dancing together, surely conspiring for my demise. I thought about the rumor passed around the art world—that the only reason Ian had picked Dick to be his dealer was because of the similar sound of their last names. No one actually knew if it was true, but I decided right then that it was, and the utter ridiculousness of such a motive made me that much more positive Ian was a great big fraud. "Kate, no! No. Oh, he's such a fraud, such a fake! I mean the whole name thing. *Reese* sounds like *Rhys!* That is so ridiculous, so annoying that he chose his representation that way!"

Perhaps doubly annoying to me, I thought, but didn't say. I had no choice in the rhyming sound of my names, and now it looked likely that the only name I'd ever see after Jane was Laine.

Instead, I reminded Kate again about my not being able to understand Ian's artwork, and about how I never liked traveling. How what I really wanted, what I really needed, was to stay home. She maintained that it was an exciting opportunity, and that I might like it. I concluded that she'd watched too many *Baby Shakespeare* videos with her daughter, and her brain had gone soft. So I said it was fine if she wasn't going to feel sorry for me, I was already feeling plenty sorry for myself. Then Kate said she had some really exciting news.

"I want to set you up with a friend of Diego's from business school. I've met him and he's great. His name is Dan. I don't know why I didn't think of it sooner. Actually Diego thought of it. I guess I'm just not used to you being single."

Me either, I thought. "Is it Dan Abrams?" I asked.

The only way I could see any point in going on a date with someone right before I was to leave New York for five months would be if it was with the very cute, in an intellectual way, legal correspondent on NBC. I think I first fell for him during all the Gore/Bush fiasco, when he was standing on the steps of some Washington, D.C., building reading the verdict really quickly, trying to figure out what was going on as he read. After the election, he got his own show where people call in and he yells at them. For Dan Abrams, Legal Correspondent, of course an exception would be made.

"No, Jane. It isn't Dan Abrams. But really, think about it. Diego thinks very highly of him, and I met him and I think he is—"

"I know. He's great."

Kate's husband Diego *is* great. He is handsome and smart and successful and Latin. Antonio Banderas as an investment banker. Kate met him on a blind date. Still, what was the point of going on a date with Diego's great friend Dan when I was leaving for so long? I asked Kate as much.

"Well, it's not really five months. You'll be back in January for two weeks, right? If you hit it off you could be e-mail pals, and he travels a lot for business. Maybe he would travel to one of the cities that you'll be in? Janie, just give it a shot. If you don't like him then you don't, and it's two hours out of your life. But you never know, he could be the one. He could wind up coming to dinner in Miami!"

Kate knew I was a sucker for the dinner-in-Miami line.

"Okay. Give him my number, but tell him I am leaving October second," I told her, hoping this great Dan looked like Diego.

The next two weeks went by in a flurry. I read and reviewed folder upon folder of travel plans, exhibition schedules, shipping schedules, media schedules, and press releases. Amanda, of course, had organized everything perfectly, but I had a lot to catch up on, and even a few things to take care of on my own. I felt more energized than I had in a long while. I even thought that maybe this trip wasn't the second worst thing ever to happen to me—then Ian came into the gallery. One of his sculptures wasn't disassembling properly, and he was thinking of leaving it in New York.

Dick decided it was my fault.

He rolled his eyes at me from the moment Ian departed until the gallery closed.

My parents invited me to a farewell dinner at Le Bilboquet, a small French bistro on the Upper East Side, and I was quite looking forward to the poulet. For some reason, my mother was very intent that we eat at Le Bilboquet. It's known not so much for its delicious Cajun-style chicken as for its loud music and throngs of transplanted Eurotrash—not at all the type of place my suburban parents would enjoy. But when I suggested Grace's, quiet and homey, and right in my neighborhood, my mother said, "Bilboquet," again, and we left it at that.

As I waited at a small table in the corner, I was thinking of how good it would be to see Mom and Dad, without the Schnauzers. My dad walked in and smiled when he saw me. I smiled back but only for a moment, because then in walked my mom, carrying Elijah. As my parents took their seats and Elijah filled the fourth chair, I didn't want to see the book my mother was pushing toward me devoted entirely to listing dog-friendly places in Manhattan. I didn't want to see how there weren't actually that many restaurants, except of course Le Bilboquet, that allowed dogs. I wanted to know why Elijah, the neediest and most high-maintenance of all my Schnauzer siblings, was joining us for dinner.

"Dear, we were just at Elijah's therapist and she thinks Elijah's eating disorder might be solved if she eats at the table," my mother told me.

I fought the urge to say that perhaps the therapist meant at the table *at home*.

"I thought the therapist suggested boiled chicken?" I asked in spite of myself.

"New therapist."

I learned that in addition to sitting at the table, the answer to Elijah's myriad dysfunctions might lie in baby food. I looked away as Mom removed a glass jar of strained carrots from her purse and set it on the table. Picking up the menu, I consoled myself with the knowledge that at least Elijah wouldn't be having her very own Poulet Cajun.

Before I knew it, all that was left of my being Jane Laine, seldom-traveling resident of New York City, was one last day at the Dick Reese Gallery and a blind date with Diego's fabulous friend, Great Dan. Victor got me an account with Hotmail as a good-bye present, so I could keep in constant contact and not be deprived of my precious e-mail. Because I was going to be on planes so often, he cleverly added that into the address—planejane6@hotmail.com. Never a fan of the blind date, Victor's enthusiasm for my date with Great Dan did not exactly rival Kate's. "It's forcing destiny," he said. I tried to explain how one good date was all it took. He smiled at me sadly, shook his head, and said "Oh, honey."

Because of how busy my last two weeks were, and because Great Dan traveled a lot himself, it had been difficult to find a time for the date. The only night we both had free was the night before I was to leave. Kate thought this was a good omen. If I didn't go out with Great Dan, she rationalized, I would just stay at home frenzied about not wanting to leave in the first place.

I tried to be optimistic.

About the date, not the trip.

Maybe all it took *was* just one good blind date. If I had learned anything from recent experience, it was that everything could change in a minute, whether you wanted it to or not. You could look at daisies and go from being a girlfriend to an ex-girlfriend. You could order the wrong size Reese's peanut butter cups and go from being a badly treated employee to an exiled, bag-and-sculpture-carrying gopher girl.

I had to believe that things could get good just as easily.

9

GET A ROOM

"I believe in low lights and trick mirrors. A person
is entitled to the lighting they need."
—Andy Warhol

On my last day in the gallery, the Velociraptor spent her morning lurking around my desk in anticipation of sitting at it while I was gone. I tried to be Zen-like and accept that if Dick wanted Amanda to sit in my spot, then that was just how it was going to be. To distract myself, I sent my new Hotmail address to everyone I knew. For the rest of the day, whenever I hit send/receive, a bon voyage message from someone would pop up.

And as a parting gift from the art gallery gods I hardly saw Dick all day.

He appeared, as if out of nowhere, only once. As always, he stood for a minute glowering at me, then left, then

intercommed to ask me again if I had all of Ian's press releases "et cetera" in order. Then the Velociraptor slithered up
to me, asking if I was excited to go.

"Not really." *Why did I tell her that? Why can't I just be
fake and enthusiastic to the point of derangement like she is?*

"Well, Jane," Amanda said, "I want to mention something. You know Dr. Ted?"

Dr. Ted is Amanda's chiropractor. She goes to see him
constantly. I went once and found the entire experience hor-
rifying; the neck twisting and back cracking left my skin crawling for days. But, yes, I knew Dr. Ted. Why was she asking?
If I looked closely, I was sure I would see little wheels of am-
bition and manipulation spinning in her head. When she first
started at the gallery I explained everything to her, and she
thanked me profusely and continuously for all of my help,
like a real team player. Then, whenever anyone asked her for
something that Dick wanted, she would smile and say, "I'm
sorry, I don't know anything about that." After which, she
would do whatever it was Dick had asked someone else to
do, and he would deem everyone not half as wonderful, talented, or vital to the gallery as Amanda.

I narrowed my eyes and said yes, I knew who Dr. Ted was.

"Well. This trip sounds so trying and well, beneath you.
It's like a valet's job, which must be *extremely* disappointing
at this point in your career. I want you to know I totally em-
pathize with you, and I really feel for you."

"Okay." I stood my ground and waited for her to get
where she was going.

"He's looking for a receptionist. Maybe that would be
better for you."

I wanted the ice age to come back and cover the earth. I thought of a million things to say but they wouldn't translate from my mind to my mouth. She and Dick were made for each other. "You have got to be kidding," I said at last, and gave her a Dick Reese eye roll. I got up and headed to the bathroom, Zen-like feelings long gone, stress creeping into my nonchiropractored neck. When I returned to my desk Amanda was gone.

Soon enough my last day at the gallery (for a while at least) came to an end. Victor winked at me as he left. I wondered why he was leaving before Dick, and assumed that he actually wasn't, that he was probably just running out for the final banana juice of the day. I had a momentary feeling of peace: for five glorious months, I wouldn't have to say good night to Dick.

Then there was Dick himself, silently taking his cape out of the closet, preparing to leave. He turned toward my desk and looked at me. I looked up from my computer and met his eyes. They got even smaller as he fingered the bow now tied loosely around his neck. He inhaled, exhaled, and then said heavily, "Good night, Jane."

"Good night, Dick."

I hit send/receive on my e-mail one last time; said good-bye to Clarissa, who enthusiastically wished me many successes on my trip and in my life; took a last look at all the white walls; and left the Dick Reese Gallery.

I put on lip gloss as I walked down Tenth Avenue. The color was called *Happy*. If only it could seep through my lips and

into my soul. I looked in my small mirror and tried to sur-
reptitiously brush my hair as I walked around a corner. Great
Dan and I were meeting at a bar in Soho, just about halfway
between my gallery and his office. I walked into the bar and
there, looking toward the doorway, was a very tall, extremely
handsome man. *Gorgeous.* Navy blue suit; red and blue tie.
Loved his suit. Loved his tie. Loved him. "Kate," I said tele-
pathically, and I was sure in Miami she heard me. "Great."

I walked over to great, gorgeous, and fabulous Dan wishing I had spent a bit more time fixing up. I put on my best
smile, tossed my hair so that it flew back behind my shoulder,
and crossed my fingers. "Dan?" I asked, flashing as many
teeth as possible and flying as much hair as I could.

"Jane? Hi. So nice to meet you." He extended his hand to
me. We shook and he began saying Diego had said so many
nice things about me. I noticed he had pretty green eyes. I
wondered why it felt like I had seen them before. Then I saw
recognition in them, and he looked sort of startled.

Instantly I stopped my shameless dental display and
ceased the hair flipping.

He didn't say anything for a full minute as we both just
stood there.

I noticed his pack of cigarettes on the bar and, as if it had
just been said, "Get a room," filled my head. Was New York
City really just a small town? Was I the only one confused
into thinking it was a very big city with *millions* of people in
it? That living here could let you be anonymous, could let
your mistakes go unseen?

"Nice to see you again, Jane."

He winked at me before asking what I wanted to drink.

What were the odds? I wanted to tell him I didn't want a drink, and that I wasn't really white trash, and that I didn't usually bum cigarettes off strangers, and that I *never* made out in the middle of a crowd in Central Park. I wanted to tell him that six weeks ago I had been normal. "Stoli Orange and soda, please," I said instead.

We each had a drink and then he said he had to meet a client for dinner and he hoped I understood. He offered me money for a taxi and I said I was fine and thanked him for the drink. The taxi driver took the FDR uptown. I looked at all the lights of the city and wondered how many other people had gone on blind dates this evening, and how many were going to end their night feeling the way I felt?

I opened the window and let the air hit my face. I turned away from the city and looked out over the East River instead. It was peaceful on that side. On the city side, there was too much. *Maybe*, I thought, *leaving New York is not the worst thing after all.*

10

REALLY, REALLY

"The moment you label something you take a step."
—Andy Warhol

The next day Ian called to suggest that we meet for lunch before leaving for the airport.

This, I thought, was bizarre.

Weren't we going to spend plenty of time together during
the next five months? I grimaced at the phone in my hand
and thought of telling him I wasn't packed yet, but not being packed would make me seem unprepared, a last-minute
type of person. He might tell Dick and then Dick would
fire me. "That sounds great, Ian. Where should I meet you?"
I asked, thinking how loath I was to start my jail sentence
of confusion and boredom any sooner than necessary. Ian
was the fountain from which all stress, humiliation, and shame

would spout during the eternity that was to be the Art Fair Project, of this I was certain.

He suggested the restaurant in the lobby of the Tribeca Grand Hotel, since we were flying out of Newark. From there we could go right through the tunnel to the airport after we ate. "I can send my driver to collect you, if you would like," he offered.

"Oh, thanks. That's really nice of you."

"Would an hour be okay, then?"

"More than enough time, thanks again."

Hanging up, I was worried. Maybe I shouldn't have accepted? Maybe having Ian send his driver doesn't fall under the umbrella of Ian "not doing anything at all"? Would I soon be getting a screaming call on my new international Dick Reese Gallery cell phone, with Dick telling me I am useless and stupid and should have taken a cab?

When I arrived at the Church Lounge in the Tribeca Grand's lobby, Ian was already seated at a table. As I approached, he stood and extended his hand to me.

"Hello there, Jane."

"Hi, Ian," I said, shaking his hand.

I wished I had said, "Hello, Ian." With his clipped consonants and precise pronunciation, Ian is the type of person who makes you want to say "hello." I'm the type of person who, when made nervous, will say the wrong thing. Every time. We talked for a minute about what time our flight was, and what time we should be sure lunch was over so we could get to the airport on time. Then we didn't have anything to talk about. Nothing. It was my fault; I should have asked about his thoughts on the Art Fair Project, or about his ideas for upcoming sculptures.

Instead, I tried to put both subjects off for as long as possible.

We ordered lunch, and Ian ordered a glass of wine. I wanted one, too, but had already said I wanted water. Not realizing Ian would be a festive, wine-drinking-at-lunch type of person, I hadn't wanted to be the only one drinking. "You know," I told the waiter, "I would love a glass, too." I turned to Ian, "Good idea. Anything to sleep on the plane."

Ian said, "On second thought, better make mine a Pellegrino." Then he looked at me with zeal in his eyes. "I want to stay up on the plane. I want to write down as many thoughts as I can about this project before we officially begin it." So the waiter crossed things out and I got my glass of wine and Ian got his water, and I was drinking alone with the greatest artistic genius of all time.

And then, horribly, he began to talk about the Art Fair Project.

I knew I couldn't put it off any longer. I had to say something. I put my wine down, and tried to think of what to say—and how to phrase it. While not understanding the larger picture that was Ian's groundbreaking talent, I did understand the basic principle of traveling around to all these different fairs. I understood that Ian wanted to experience it all, record it all, and comment on it all. Apparently he was keeping some sort of journal and something—a sculpture maybe?—was going to come out of that. "So, Ian," I started slowly. "Please explain to me, are you writing these thoughts down just as sort of a journal, or are they, in some way, going to be incorporated into your work?" I wished I had left out the *just* and the *sort of*. I wished I had something smarter to say and I wished that my glass of wine weren't already half empty.

"Well, indeed," Ian exclaimed. "Absolutely, yes. I believe positively everything that anyone experiences will become inextricably incorporated into their work, whatever that work may be. So, in that sense, yes, all my thoughts are somehow incorporated into my work, as I am sure all your thoughts somehow make it into your work. But more specifically, what the writing is going to focus on is . . ."

I should have listened. But I didn't; instead I wondered if all my thoughts really made it into my work. Maybe that was why I wasn't very happy with my work? But weren't a lot of the unhappy thoughts *because of* work?

Ian kept talking.

I smiled and said, "mmm," and he started drawing a little diagram on a napkin for me. *No, not a diagram. Please.* I heard "the interaction of objects and forms" and "dynamism" and "interplay." I watched his lips moving. *Blah, blah, blah.* I found myself thinking, *Is Ian's real genius that he knows how to fake it?* I narrowed my eyes. *Maybe nothing Ian says about his artwork or even himself is true.* Maybe Ian doesn't come from London at all, but from Idaho. And not the potato part of Idaho, but the crazy, inbred parents locking their children up in a cabin, away from schooling and vitamins, guarding 'em safe with a twelve-gauge shotgun, part of Idaho.

"There. Yes. Just one more," Ian said softly, as he worked on his drawing.

I leaned back in my chair and looked up at the walkways above the bar. The Church Lounge is in the center of the lobby so you can look up at all the balconies and hallways that lead to the hotel rooms. Kind of like an atrium. I don't know if it was an effort to be in accordance with proper fire codes, but all around the bar and above it, every few feet, I saw bright red exit signs.

They seemed to be closing in on me.

Exit, Exit, Exit wherever I looked.

After lunch, Ian's driver took us through the tunnel to Newark Airport and left us. We brought our bags up to the check-in counter at International Departures and handed our tickets to the woman behind it. She smiled at Ian but it was a courtesy smile, not a smile because he was famous. Here, he wasn't famous. In the airport with people who don't care about art, who don't run around Chelsea foraging for ground-breaking, spectacular, important, and earth-shattering artists, Ian was just someone wearing a very loud shirt. It was the first time I ever saw him not being the center of attention. The absence of people coming up to tell him how great he was, or how meaningful something he had done was, or to congratulate him on being Ian Rhys-Fitzsimmons, made me feel a little less nervous.

"Okay, Mr. Rhys-Fitzsimmons," said the check-in woman. "You'll be in seat 2B. And Miss Laine, you are in 37E."

"Excuse me?" said Ian.

"Yes, 2B and 37E," repeated the check-in woman.

"I am in first class and you are in coach?" Ian asked me.

He seemed concerned, embarrassed. I thought about Amanda, making plane reservations and asking for a middle-of-the-row E seat, a seat with so many people on either side who you have to wake up in order to go to the bathroom, and wake up again when you come back. "Yes, it looks that way," I told him.

"Well, that's ridiculous," Ian said.

He took out his frequent flier card and asked if there could be an upgrade.

Check-in woman told him no. As he asked about buying a first-class ticket, I thought how odd it was that this Dick-inspired segregation was disturbing to him. Thinking about Dick, I knew he would be beside himself, would freak out, if gallery money was used to buy a last-minute first-class ticket. And if, God forbid, Dick found out that Ian used his own money . . . I knew too well how quickly Dick would fly his broomstick to London to spread torture and misery.

"Ian, really, thank you so much but I am fine with my seat," I told him.

"I'm sorry," said check-in woman. "Business First is completely sold out on this flight." She held up a hand. "But what I can do," she continued, glancing at her computer screen, "is switch 37E to a bulkhead row. How is 7D? The seats on either side are empty."

I nodded enthusiastically and Ian smiled and she changed my ticket.

I thanked Ian and felt awkward and embarrassed, then thanked check-in woman.

"You're welcome," she told me. Then she said, "Mr. Rhys-Fitzsimmons," as we started to walk away, "I am a *huge* fan of your work."

"Thank you. Very much," he said.

We headed toward the gate, and I was very glad the seating arrangement was worked out, and that soon we would be in different cabins. I would be separated from all the formality and awkwardness, and I could drink wine until I fell asleep. But just as I was beginning to relax, Ian said that *he* would sit in the bulkhead seat and I could have his first-class ticket.

With veiled references to Dick and the fact that he would be enraged, I spent the next half hour convincing Ian that really, I wanted to sit in coach. I told him I was tired, that all I was going to do was sleep. That I was only five-four, and with an empty seat beside me I could stretch out. Granted, at five-sevenish Ian doesn't fall under the general heading of tall, but I didn't mention that. Instead, I told him I worked for Dick, and needed to do things the way he had planned them. I tried to gauge whether Ian would update Dick on everything that happened. There wasn't any way to tell. "I *want* to sit there," I repeated. "*Really,* really."

"*Really,* really?" he asked.

"Yes, Ian. *Really,* really."

"No." He smiled and it looked like he was going to laugh. "I wasn't asking you if you were sure you wanted to sit there. I was asking about the '*really,* really' as a colloquial phrase," he explained.

I, in turn, explained that "*really,* really" was just like "very, very" or "super, extremely" or "undoubtedly, one hundred percent." It was unconditional, I told him. It meant that you completely, utterly wanted to do something, that you were not hindered by any doubts whatsoever.

He smiled again and finally, mercifully, he agreed to stay in his seat. I had a little time to get away from him, so I hurried to the newsstand and bought *People, Us, Entertainment Weekly, Allure* and *In Style*. I grabbed the October *Art News* to put on top of the pile, to hide the magazines beneath.

11

MATH FUNDAMENTALS

"The less something has to say,
the more perfect it is."
—Andy Warhol

The bulkhead wasn't half bad, and I set about organizing my magazines. 7C and 7E were empty so I had space on either side of me. A nice, quiet-looking lady was in 7F chatting with a guy about my age in 7G. That was fine—they were far enough away for me to get some privacy.

After takeoff I felt scared. I always do, because really, you've just been listening to all the things about crashes and evacuations and you have to watch that movie with the flight attendant proudly showing you her emergency flotation device and disaster situation oxygen mask. And also in the bulkhead you have extra responsibilities in case of a crash; you have to help people get out of the plane before it fills up with the Atlantic Ocean. They actually tell you that you can switch seats if you aren't comfortable performing such duties. But if it was a matter of helping people get out of the plane alive or squishing into 37E for six hours, I was prepared to help my fellow travelers.

I read *People* for about ten minutes to calm my nerves, declined the headphones because the one movie choice for the coach people was something about robots, and decided to get some sleep. I put my magazines and my bottle of water next to me in 7C, reclined my seat, got my blanket all unfolded, and closed my eyes. I had that nice cloudy feeling that I was going to fall right to sleep. *How nice it will be to sleep the whole way to London . . .*

"Are these yours?"

It was loud. It was screechy and it had a southern accent. I opened my eyes to see a large woman in a purple muumuu-type top, black leggings, and running shoes pointing to my magazine, water, and handbag. "Yes?" She handed my things to me and sat down in 7C. I could feel my peacefulness slipping away as she overflowed into territory that clearly belonged to seat 7D. I could see that the man she had been sitting with—her husband maybe—was spreading out in the two seats from whence she had come. I had to do something. "Um. I was all organized here," I said, hoping perhaps she would not want to disrupt my organization and would go away.

"Well," she said too loudly. She took her ring-addled hand and tossed my magazines from my lap onto the floor in front of me. "We can just get reorganized, can't we?" She smiled at me as if we had to become very best friends. "Sue Anne Bellefield." She extended her hand after taking my water bottle from me and putting it, too, on the floor where it proceeded to roll away. Dehydration and overcrowding clearly in my future, I didn't want conversation to be as well.

"Jane Laine." I said, and as soon as I shook her hand, I pulled my blanket up, closed my eyes, wished I had asked for headphones, tried to pretend I was going to sleep, and tried to believe that, somehow, I still could. Why did she have to come and ruin all the bulkhead happiness, take away any chance of spreading out across the seats later on? *Why, muumuu lady from somewhere south, why?*

"Sue Anne Bellefield," I heard again.

I felt Sue Anne Bellefield leaning over me, pressing against me, climbing into my lap. I opened my eyes and saw that she wasn't actually climbing into my lap, which was definitely a good thing, but was still leaning across me, extending a soft, fleshy arm to the quiet-seeming, but actually not-so-quiet woman in 7F.

"Riva Washington. So nice to meet you," said 7F quite happily.

This was bad, very bad. Why was nice, quiet lady over there not acting the way she looked? Why were people, with alarming frequency, so rarely the way they seemed? Wasn't it enough for her to chat away with chatty 7G?

"I love your accent, Sue Anne. And what a pretty name, Bellefield. Where are you from?"

"Atlanta, Georgia! And you?"

I knew, but didn't want to admit, that these two were in it for the long haul; these two would talk to each other the whole way. I kept my eyes closed, hoping that every sentence would be the last, praying that they had nothing in common.

Filtering through the screaming in my mind, I learned both Sue Anne and Riva were teachers. Both had spent over twenty years in the public school system and apparently, this plane ride was the perfect, long-awaited opportunity to discuss the myriad differences between New York City and Atlanta school systems. And even better, Gabe, Riva's friend over in 7G, from Salt Lake City, taught Sunday school classes at his Mormon tabernacle! *Why? Why were they here? Why were they going to London?* Occasionally, I almost fell asleep, but right when I got to that beautiful instant when everything is about to not be there anymore, I would be jolted awake by one of them:

". . . lesson plan!"

". . . curriculum!"

". . . learning retention!"

I snapped. "I'm just curious—are any of you ever going to go to *sleep?* Because if you are going to *keep talking* then I need to go find somewhere else."

I felt embarrassed as the words came out of my mouth, but I couldn't help myself. They looked at me and looked at each other. Sue Anne called me Dolly, and told me they "din't know that right just yet" but if I wanted to I could switch seats with Gabe.

"Gabe, doll, you don't mind that, d'you?" She winked once at Gabe and then rolled her eyes at Riva, revealing herself to be another minion of the Antichrist.

I took my blanket and my magazines from the floor, gathered up my bag, and went in search of a different seat. Two hours into the flight and all the passengers had stretched out across two seats, some of them across three and four, and fallen asleep. As I got toward the back of the plane, I noticed an especially lucky person stretched out across all five seats. I didn't want to look at the row number. I was sure I would see the number 37, looking at me and laughing. I wondered if anyone would mind if I just lay quietly down in the aisle.

"Ma'am, you need to be in your seat with your seat belt fastened," a flight attendant said, pointing at the lit Fasten Seat Belt sign. I made my way back to my seat, calculating the hours until we reached London. Everyone in coach was asleep except for Sue Anne, Riva, and Gabe, who were still having a grand old time with the subject of New Math.

As I got back into my seat they glared at me.

An eternity later, we landed at Heathrow Airport.

I was sure I wouldn't be able to carry all of Ian's belongings in the sleep-deprived, stressed-out, completely frantic, teeth-gnashing state I was currently in. Sue Anne Bellefield—who had not returned to her original seat for landing—and her new favorite people had talked for the duration of the flight. I felt as if I had been licking a block of salt for the past six hours.

"Cheers, Jane!" sang Ian, smiling broadly as he greeted me, looking refreshed and energetic. I didn't want to know whether he had stayed up the whole flight working; he certainly looked like he'd had a full night's sleep in the luxury of his quiet, peaceful, first-class seat, awakening perhaps to a lovely mimosa and a brioche.

Fuck off, Ian! "Hi, Ian," I said and didn't care that I hadn't said, "Hello, Ian."

I started walking with him toward immigration. As we each went to different lines, one for citizens of the United Kingdom and one for visitors, Ian told me he would be waiting for me on the other side of the pass-through that led to baggage claim. Through the headache and dizziness that was engulfing me, I thought about how he was going to point out his bags so I could carry them on one of those airport carts. That's what anyone who travels with Dick has to do. But when I came through immigration, Ian was waiting with a cart. He got his own bags from the baggage carousel and when I went to get mine he actually cut in, quite politely, to grab them, and then he pushed all our luggage on the cart himself. It wasn't the sherpa-like scenario I had been envisioning for the past two weeks at all.

12

MEET ME ON MADDOX STREET

*"Over the years I've been more successful at dealing with love
than with jealousy. I get jealousy attacks all the time."*
—Andy Warhol

The London Contemporary Art Fair
London, England

It wasn't until we were through customs and Ian had carted
our bags outside to the taxi line—or queue as it is called in
England—and we were on our way into London, that it hit
me. I was in a foreign city! A beautiful, elegant foreign city.
The taxi was clean, and the driver was nice to us, and he sat
on the right side of the car. The road signs were unknown;
the cars looked different and the advertisements were all unfamiliar. I thought for the first time that this trip might actually be good. It might, as Kate had predicted, be fun.

Then Ian asked me, "What hotel are you staying at?"

It was first class and 37E all over again. I could practically hear Dick telling Amanda to book Ian at the Connaught, or the Sanderson if he was feeling modernist, and to put me in some prostitute-infested motel that rented rooms by the hour. I reminded myself that this was not some fabulous holiday. That even though Dick wasn't physically with us, slithering and snapping at me, he was making sure his hateful presence would be felt. I took out one of Amanda's many folders to be sure I remembered the hotel correctly, and to notice again that it was so insignificant it didn't even have a name, just an address. I looked over at Ian, who was quietly waiting for an answer. "Number 5 Maddox Street," I told him.

"Oh, interesting choice. Very posh address. Quite unique, actually. Don't know if I picture you there, but convenient nonetheless to Duke Street, where the gallery is, and easy enough to get to the Business Design Centre, where the fair is."

Was Ian being funny, or was 5 Maddox Street really a posh address? Or did he not picture me there because he couldn't see me trotting around with English prostitutes? I didn't want to ask questions—and why did he feel he had to tell me that the gallery was on Duke Street and the fair was at the Business Design Centre? Didn't he think I had prepared at all? Didn't he at least see all of the labeled folders I was carrying? If 5 Maddox Street was so unique, then why wasn't he staying there, too?

"Where are you staying?" *The Connaught, Claridges, the Ritz?*

"Well I can't say I would mind staying at 5 Maddox myself.

But, actually, I keep a flat here in London. So, for this leg of the trip, I won't be at the hotel."

As he made sure I had his address and phone number, our taxi turned onto a quiet street, stopped at Number 5, and both the driver and Ian got out to help me with my bags. I watched Ian and wondered how I would manage to change our dynamic so that I was doing what I was supposed to be doing—taking care of him. We said good-bye and arranged to meet in two hours to head over to the art fair. The taxi left and I wheeled my bag over the curb toward a black door with No. 5 Maddox Street written on it. There was no awning, no doorman, just an intercom. Cautiously, I buzzed.

"Hello, do you have a reservation?" asked a very pleasant English voice.

Even though the voice was lovely, talking through an intercom made me uncomfortable. For a fleeting, jet-lagged moment I wondered if I'd been signed into an international prostitution ring by Amanda and Dick . . . and possibly Ian. I looked down the street and it was very nice and very chic and didn't *seem* seedy, so clearly I must have been wrong. Then I remembered Heidi Fleiss, and before her the Mayflower Madam, and figured I probably was very, very right. "Yes, Laine? It's for one month. Jane Laine?"

I was buzzed into the lobby of Number 5 Maddox Street.

It was, for lack of a more descriptive word, fabulous.

It was so many things, all melded together in the most Zen-like combination, from the bamboo floors and the huge James Bond movie–like aquarium, to the high-tech flat-screen computers at the reception desk. The sleek lines and the peaceful quiet that permeated the lobby all worked together to make me unsure of whether I was in a superhip bachelor pad or a Japanese spa. Either way, I was *really,* really happy to be there.

Check-in was easy. Then I went quickly up one flight of stairs to my room; actually it was a suite. It was decorated in muted colors and kept the same high-tech-meets-tranquility feeling achieved so flawlessly in the lobby. As I looked around at all the gadgets and chocolates and beiges and creams, I felt bad for thinking Amanda had booked me into a flea-ridden motel. Even with all the gadgets, the room felt very peaceful. I noticed a dark brown cashmere throw on my bed and as I walked into the mini kitchen, opening cabinets, I saw it was well stocked with groceries. Opening the freezer, I saw three different kinds of Ben & Jerry's ice cream. *Yeah, Amanda!*

Unpacking was a snap. I ate a bag of "crisps" that I thought were potato chips, and was happy to realize I had an hour and a half to take a nap. I wondered why Ian had said he didn't picture me here? Was it because he didn't think I was fabulous? Or sleek? Or Feng Shui Zen? Then, somehow, some of the Buddhist calm permeating the room soaked into me; I decided he didn't picture me here because I wasn't a swinging London bachelor. *Because I am a lady,* I thought, *not because I'm not cool.* I curled up on the sleek cream couch with the cashmere throw over me and I didn't think about not understanding Ian's art or that he was really from Idaho. I closed my eyes and could still see the perfect placement of every object in the room. Everything got quieter and quieter and more Zen-like and Zen-like until there wasn't anything at all except for softness.

It seemed only seconds later that the phone rang and it was Ian, in the lobby, ready to go over to the fair.

Even though I have worked at many art fairs over the years, I haven't ever been part of the setup. I've always been back at the gallery, enjoying Dick's absence and helping Clarissa answer all the calls he makes, most of which are complaining or scolding calls for me. James Sloane, the owner of the gallery where we would be exhibiting later in the month (and also one of the top dealers of Contemporary art in London) had arranged for some people to help us, so happily I wouldn't be lugging sculptures around, not in a wagon or over my head.

Instead, art handlers, a special moving person, and Ian himself went back and forth with dollies and handcarts, wheeling covered pieces of sculptures to the booth and situating them according to a graph paper diagram on which Ian had figured out exactly where he wanted everything. There were four sculptures in our booth, the focal point of the group being a large piece Ian had recently completed, *Untitled #6*. Never before seen by the public, it was already being lauded as Ian's greatest artistic achievement to date.

I spent most of my time on a ladder adjusting lights. It was hot and sweaty, but also novel and enjoyable. I looked out over the temporary partitions and saw all the other galleries setting up and felt a familiarity within all the newness. Inside these walls, under the bright lights, I could have been in London or New York. It could have been October or June. There was something comforting about that just as much as there was something creepy. The air felt the same as it always did; the transient tension that always buzzed around at art fairs is the same no matter what big open space it's occupying. But then, there were also things that made it feel different. These changes, such as our booth location—we weren't placed front and center as we usually were—and the complete absence of endless complaints from Dick made it clear I was far from home.

With London being Ian's birthplace and where he grew up, the city takes a special pride in his achievements. Though I wondered if maybe there wasn't an underlying resentment—Ian had left London, taken off for the States, becoming as much a part of American culture as of British, perhaps even more so. Maybe behind all the greetings of *"I am so honored to meet you, Mr. Rhys-Fitzsimmons"* and *"Welcome home"* and *"Feels good to be back, doesn't it,"* London in fact wished that Ian had stayed home so the greatest artist of all time would be a local. As James Sloane strode into our booth, I wondered if he counted all the money he had never made as a result of Ian being represented by the Dick Reese Gallery in New York, and not by the Sloane Gallery in London.

"Ah. Mr. Rhys-Fitzsimmons. Welcome home. Feels good to be back in London, doesn't it?" he said, patting Ian's shoulder. He did not seem at all bitter or resentful. He probably didn't count money he didn't have, but was rather getting ready to count all the money he was going to make from the first gallery exhibit of the Ian Rhys-Fitzsimmons Art Fair Project tour. James Sloane—and the dealers hosting us in the other cities—would not only receive all the press and buzz that came with being associated with Ian, but they would also get a small percentage of any sales made at their galleries.

"James. Great to be here, great to see you," Ian said enthusiastically and then turned to me and smiled, "James, this is Jane Laine; she's here with me from the Dick Reese Gallery."

I got down from the ladder and held out my hand. "Hello. It's nice to meet you," I said and was glad that "Hello" had made an appearance rather than the usual "Hi" that always barged in. As our hands touched, I looked at James Sloane's face and was reminded very much of a water rat. He had a reddish hue to his skin, thin blond hair, and liquid gray eyes. A long skinny nose and an upper lip that protruded slightly made me picture twitching whiskers pointing down toward his bow tie and tweed suit.

"Mr. Sloane," he said haughtily, quickly turning back to Ian.

There must be some secret summit where prominent art dealers gather to plan how to retain their power. A key part of the strategy has to be never act like a human being. Mr. Sloane walked with Ian to the other side of the booth and now was squinting at a sculpture. "Ian, Ian, this is just spectacular. Great, great work. Majestic." Ian was gesturing animatedly, and Mr. Sloane levered his head up and down in an accelerated "yes" motion. "Oh, and Ian, Imogen is thrilled you'll be at the dinner next week. We are both greatly looking forward to having you," he added with a purse-lipped smile. I could positively see long rat whiskers twitching.

"Yes. I'm looking forward to it as well. It's been a long time since I've seen Imogen, it'll be lovely to catch up," Ian answered as he and Mr. Sloane headed out of our booth.

•   •   •

Even though we weren't in the "very-first-glimpse-of-a-gallery" position, we didn't have a bad spot by any means. We were close to the front, and definitely would never be overlooked. Another something that was different, that would *never* happen in New York: we were situated right next to our top competitor, Kratsch Gallery. All the brain aneurysms Dick had thrown in his lifetime to date would pale in comparison to what would go on were he here and subjected to working next to the almost-as-successful-as-himself Karina Kratsch.

He would scream that two dealers of similar material cannot be so close to each other, as if it were an affront to aesthetics and rhythm. As if it were a concern to him that the fair visitor experience diversity. But the truth is, Dick would never want to be anywhere near Karina Kratsch's booth for the sole reason that her presence makes him squirm. I watched the Kratsch Gallery being set up next to us, feeling fortunate he was not standing there berating me for not knowing the plans of the London art fair organizers.

At seven, at last, it seemed everything was in order.

I tried to calculate what time it was in New York. In the past day, I had only slept for an hour and a half. I felt disheveled and exhausted and dirty, and I hoped Ian was ready to go. I ducked into the booth closet to get my bag, hoping he wouldn't keep me there to look at graph paper, or talk about experiences going into work or objects fitting together. Emerging, I saw that, thankfully, Ian was also gathering up his things.

"Well, Jane. Thanks for everything. I think we are in great shape," he said, not seeming tired at all.

"Yes, I do, too. I'm going to head back to my hotel. Unless you need anything else?" I asked, hoping he didn't.

"Excited to be in London, then?"

"Yes, definitely," I said, hoping against hope that his next sentence would be about seeing me tomorrow.

"What sort of things do you want to do while you're here?"

Oh no, I thought, visions of my hotel room rapidly eclipsed by an image of myself climbing the Tower of London with Ian right behind me.

"I'd like to go to Audrey," I blurted, feeling heat flood my face the moment the words escaped. *Audrey? What about the National Gallery? The Tate? Or Buckingham Fucking Palace?* No. I said Audrey, some London restaurant that had opened an outpost in New York about a year ago and was probably closed here by now, or at the very least, very, very over. *Where,* I wondered, *had that even come from?*

I was thankful then that he was so gracious. Even though he was probably thinking it as he smiled at me quizzically, he was far too nice to say out loud that I was a big, big moron.

"Ahhhh. Zare you are Ian, Dahling."

It came from behind me and unless it was Zsa Zsa Gabor, there was only one person it could be. She walked down the aisle and into our booth as if she were gliding on a catwalk. Her hips swayed back and forth and she kept one hand sliding in rhythm across her thigh as she made her way forward. Her shoulders were thrown back and her lips were in a permanent pout. Her black turtleneck dress hugged her very tall, curvy, model-like figure perfectly. She had on fishnet stockings and heels that had to be four inches high; definitely Manolo Blahnik. She looked like she had just stepped out of

Vogue. She always looked like that. For Karina Kratsch, every day is a runway day.

"Karina!" Ian seemed genuinely happy to see her. Were they friends?

"Dahling. Zee booth looks fabulous. *Fabulous,* dahling. Zee girls in my gallery, zay take so long to set everything. Zay are not done but I say I cannot keep Ian waiting for me, so I leave zem." She was very breathy. Either she has reverse asthma, or she knows she is just the sexiest sex kitten ever. She seemed exasperated, as if she had been working hard all day.

But how could you be working hard and still look so perfect?

Likely zee girls did everything while she breathed at them.

Ian asked me twice if I was okay getting back to the hotel. Karina was nice enough, said, "Helloo zare, Jane," and didn't ask me to call her Ms. Kratsch. Mostly she just kept looking at Ian the way someone on a diet might look at a ham. *Is it odd that Ian is going to dinner with Karina?* Maybe.

"Well then, thanks again, Jane. I'll see you here tomorrow morning," Ian said.

As he and Karina walked away, I noticed how she placed her hand in the middle of his back. There was something about the gesture that made me think maybe Ian and Karina were actually more than friends.

13

HAVE YOU BEEN WORKING OUT?

"No matter how good you are, if you're not
promoted right you won't be remembered."
—Andy Warhol

"Mr. Rhys-Fitzsimmons has always been very interested in
the interrelation of objects," I said over and over the next
morning, as I stood near the chrome desk we had set up in
the front corner of the booth, passing out press releases for
the London press preview. When people from newspapers
and magazines asked me about Ian's work, mostly they
wanted to know when a specific work was finished, or what
its price was. Since we were on the very first stop of our tour,
it was easy enough to keep my ignorance of the work hidden
by rattling off destinations and repeating certain phrases. I
carefully repeated phrases from our press releases, saying
"the impact of the art fairs on Mr. Rhys-Fitzsimmons'

work," "the commercial and conceptual goals of Mr. Rhys-Fitzsimmons," and "the varied and similar reactions to the artist's work in different cities," again and again.

As the day moved on and reporters returned for a second look or to ask something about a sculpture, I found myself saying things like, "The dynamic between these two shapes is really quite fascinating." My favorite line became, "It's about the funneling of extant experiences into actual events." I was speaking in alien code, but as the words came easier and the question marks fell off the ends of my sentences, amazingly, people started to nod and agree with me. All these nodding people thought I had said something important. I tried to memorize exactly how I had phrased things, to remember how to say them again.

In an effort to continue the positive feelings, I avoided talking with Ian about his art. *He* would be able to tell that I simply didn't get it. Avoiding him during the press preview proved to be quite easy; he spent most of it blinking in the flashes of a thousand cameras and answering many, many more questions than were asked of me. Also, whenever there was a lull, two girls who would be doing the PR for the art fairs would come to the booth, fawn all over Ian, smile at him, and throw their hair around.

I'd seen them before, these PR girls.

They worked for Cotlar & Lawrence, a public relations firm art fairs hire to take care of publicity and opening parties. They are always sashaying around with clipboards, tittering on about what story they are pushing to what paper. They compliment Ian endlessly saying things like "The Modern" instead of the Museum of Modern Art or "The Fall" instead of the Fall Art Fair. It is clear they firmly believe they know much more about what is in and cool and hip and now, than anybody else. All throughout the day, every time they left our booth, they seemed to pop right back in again.

"Ian! I'm sure in tomorrow's *Mail* you'll be featured in the article on the Contemporary," the thin, blond one said.

"Ian, Ian, Ian. You just have to *promise* you'll come to dinner with us tomorrow? *Please?*" the not as thin, not as blond one said, then added, "Did I tell you how great you look? Have you been working out?"

"Yes, have you been working out?" thinner, blonder parroted.

Icky PR bimbos. I would be seeing them many more times, at every fair over the next five months. Ian blushed and nodded his head and made dinner plans with them. I know promotion and publicity is a big part of all of this, but *still.* Then, for the second time in as many days, I wondered about Ian's romantic involvement. *Are Ian and the PR girls more than friends?*

As the press corps left and preparations for the opening-night party began, I put the image of the PR bimbos out of my mind. Ian went home to change, sure to return with bright colors and stripes and patterns. I headed back to my hotel in a clean London taxi. As I watched all the unfamiliar sights go by, I looked forward to the month ahead, to seeing the changing of the guard at Buckingham Palace, to going to the Tate Gallery and to St. James Park and to having tea at Browns. There was something very reassuring about looking out a window and seeing a city and thinking about all the things I wanted to do, rather than seeing a city and thinking about everything that hadn't gone the way I would have liked.

Gwyneth Paltrow has been quoted as saying that if her hair isn't straight she feels like she has zero sex appeal. If frizzy hair can do that to Gwyneth's self-image, just imagine what it can do to mine. My attempt at trying to look fancy and flawless for the opening party—to look just like Karina Kratsch, in fact—was hindered somewhat by time constraints, and severely by the very disagreeable London weather.

As I arrived back at the Business Design Centre, however, I was somehow able to put bad-hair thoughts aside. Waiting for Ian and the throngs of his black-tie fans to arrive, it was gratifying to think I wouldn't spend the whole night in the closet. I wouldn't even have to think about mini Reese's peanut butter cups, because Ian wasn't interested in the peanut butter cup concept. In fact, he had said to leave them in the closet. "Yes," he said when I emerged from the closet earlier that day, bag in hand. "Let's leave them, shall we?" I'd looked up quickly, wondering if those few words were a gesture of solidarity, proof that Ian really wasn't on the same de- mented wavelength as Dick. But he didn't meet my gaze; he was already staring back at his graph paper charts, thinking about something else, not indicating at all that he and I were bonded in mutual disregard of Dick's Reese's peanut butter cup fetish.

Still, I thought it was great. Or super, as he would have said.

I enjoyed the opening much more than any other opening

of an art fair before. I didn't recognize nearly as many of the people; most of the dealers were new to me. I didn't know their peculiarities, their irrational perspectives, their possible similarities to Dick. All the English accents, all the subdued, polished manners made it seem more sophisticated and, in a way, much more important than any previous opening I'd ever attended.

Ian, much subdued himself, wore a dark blue suit with a dark gray shirt and a dark blue tie. The slim suit, fitted perfectly to his frame, still had that European, very "Ian" look to it, but with less visual volume, less-fighting fabrics. As I watched him, surrounded frequently by the blond hair of the PR bimbos, and then occasionally by the even blonder hair of Karina Kratsch, for the first time I didn't think he looked like a caricature. It was an odd feeling.

Throughout the evening, the PR girls came and went; Karina sauntered over occasionally and said things to Ian while he nodded in agreement. I concentrated on saying all the sentences I had practiced earlier in the day, and was happy to see people nodding in agreement with me, too. I explained that yes, the Art Fair Project consisted of an art fair followed by a two-week gallery exhibition in each of the five cities we were visiting. Ian Rhys-Fitzsimmons was going to spend the first part of the art fair at the booth, and would then go to a studio and work on new art during the second part of the fair. He'd be back again for the opening of the exhibition at the Sloane Gallery, and then would leave again to "pursue his creativity." We'd go to Rome and he'd do the same again. One week on, one week off.

A brilliant artist working on his art for one week, and

then sitting around in art fair booths and exhibition rooms for a week straight, speaking knowledgeably about how vital and important and significant his art is . . . Listening to myself talk, I realized that in a weird sort of way, Ian, with all of his accomplishments, had freely chosen to have the same job as me. Ian had chosen to be a gallery girl.

Maybe I should tell him it wasn't the best choice he could make?

I looked around the booth, through the milling, fawning collectors, and saw only Ian. Just Ian Rhys-Fitzsimmons, world-renowned artist, and me. I'd considered this trip a punishment; yet maybe it was the most interesting and unique experience I had ever been part of? It was such a great opportunity—the more I thought of it, the more I absolutely couldn't believe Dick had sent me. Right then I felt lucky.

I felt so good standing there on my own, doing my job.

14

BELGIAN BEER, BUSY, BOREDOM, AND BIG TEETH

"I like boring things."

—Andy Warhol

I sold a sculpture at the opening party.

Even though sculptures sell on opening nights all the time—and Ian Rhys-Fitzsimmons sculptures sell more often than that—it was exciting. In New York, there were times when I'd almost sold something, but Dick would always step in and take over. Then when the deal closed, he would put his hands on his chubby waist, shake his hips, lift his hands with his arms bent at the elbows, and do his "I-Made-a-Sale" dance. He would leer and preen, barely able to say, "Shhh," to Clarissa when she drew in her breath and exclaimed, "YOU SOLD IT, DICK!" as though nothing had ever been sold before.

Selling something without Dick made my night.

. . .

Unfortunately, in the week that followed, nothing else sold.

Granted, there were only three other sculptures, and plenty of people took literature and information and inquired about prices, but no one made an offer on anything, not even a low one. The grand *Untitled #6* stood proudly in the middle of our booth, and everyone praised it and admired it and marveled at it, but no one seemed "comfortable," as they say, with the price tag. It was the biggest one ever on a Rhys-Fitzsimmons sculpture. And Dick didn't care about the sculpture that I did sell; in fact, he never even mentioned it. When he called each day, he would immediately ask if the others had sold.

"No," I would answer, "but—"

"Whataboutsix?" he'd snap.

"No," I'd have to tell him again, and wouldn't even try to add more.

"Let me speak to Ian. Is he there?"

"Ian, Dick's on the line," I'd say with relief as I handed over the venomous object Dick's voice had transformed the phone into. I would then leave the booth so I wouldn't have to listen to Ian thank Dick for all the compliments he slathered on him. Also, I wouldn't be around should Dick decide he had something further he wished to discuss. Much better for Ian to take a message. Then whatever command I was given was relayed in a nicer way.

Ian wasn't concerned that the sculptures weren't selling; in fact he was actually quite interested that they weren't. The way that he saw it, any resistance or lack of activity was still part of his art: everything that happened, he told me, from

concept to completion belonged to—and added further meaning to—the Art Fair Project. He explained this one day, toward
the end of the first week. There was something else, too, but
I tuned out. Not intentionally, but as he was speaking I remembered that he'd be leaving after the weekend to work on
his sculptures, and write in his journals, and conceptualize
his concepts in the countryside. It just didn't seem possible
that we'd been in London for a week already, and that it was
almost time for him to go. I hadn't had any time for tea with
cute little sandwiches and clotted cream, or for antiquing on
Portobello Road, or shopping on Sloane Street like Diana did
before she became Princess. No time at all. Most nights I just
went home and ordered room service in my sleek hotel room,
by myself.

Ian, on the other hand, went out with the PR bimbi on
two different nights, and one evening I left before him and on
my way out I passed Karina heading toward our booth. He
also went to that dinner party Mr. Sloane had talked about,
the one someone named Imogen was throwing. Possibly he
stayed home for at least one night, though I couldn't be sure
because we never talked about what we did when we weren't
at work. In fact, if it wasn't about work, we didn't talk much
at all. Ian was always very pleasant when he was in the
booth, and he often made witty, very British comments about
things that, in spite of myself, I found entertaining. But other
than his comments and my laughing at them, there wasn't
much said between us. So he caught me completely off guard
when he asked if I'd like to join him for dinner.

It was a Friday night. Saturday the fair would be twice as
crowded and we'd be at our booth for more hours than

usual. I'd been toying with the idea of going out to dinner by myself, but I felt kind of like a loser. I had just decided that if I was going to be one of those sad people out to dinner all alone, gazing forlornly into space while sipping a glass of wine, I'd better test it out on a weeknight when it was less crowded. And also I definitely needed to get a book to read, to bring with me. So I said, "That'd be nice," immediately, surprised and actually happy for the company.

We left the fair and headed to a restaurant Ian said was one of his favorites. I was picturing a very fancy, very trendy place, all white and chrome, with bored, condescending waiters, the type of place Dick favors. When we got there, we took a wrought-iron elevator down into a cavernous, boisterous space with rows of long tables with long benches on either side. It was casual and welcoming, and I was surprised. As we were shown to a section of long table that wasn't already occupied, it occurred to me that maybe I should occasionally acknowledge that Dick and Ian might not be exactly the same, despite the "Reese" and "Rhys" rhyme.

It wasn't until the waiter handed us our menus that I realized where we were.

Ian had taken me to Audrey.

Audrey—the one place I had idiotically said I wanted to see in London. I tried to think quickly of how to convey that there were plenty of very erudite and intellectual attractions in London I was more interested in. Then it occurred to me that maybe he'd taken me to Audrey to mock me and my small-mindedness. But he wasn't smirking an evil Dick-like smirk at all, and when he grinned across the table at me it was so warm and contagious I felt all of the tightness I'd been carrying in my chest since I'd learned I'd be traveling with him finally melt. Our eyes met and I grinned back at him. It was the first real smile I'd ever smiled at him, the first time it wasn't forced, or uncomfortable, or nervous, or guarded or just plain scared.

"Cheers, Jane," he said and picked up his empty glass.

"Cheers, Ian," I said picking up my own and touching it to his.

Over Belgian beers and mussels and French fries, everything between us seemed different. It was casual, normal even, or at least much more so than ever before. We talked about Ian's trip to Yorkshire, and how the second week of the art fair would be just like the first, although probably not as busy. He was so friendly I almost forgot I thought he was secretly a fake and a fraud; I decided to ask him if it was true, if the reason Dick Reese was his dealer was based solely on the sound of his name.

"That would be rather silly, wouldn't it?" he said.

I finished up the last of my fries, knowing he hadn't really answered me.

Another sculpture sold that weekend, bringing in plenty of money to the gallery, and adding further validity to the Art Fair Project and Ian's reputation. All Dick could say to me over the transatlantic phone line, though, was "Whatabout-six" and "LetmespeaktoIan."

After manic activity for two days the weekend was over, and Ian said good-bye and, "Many thanks, Jane. Super job." With a smile, and after shaking my hand, he was off to meet his car to Yorkshire, his plaid pants a colorful blur as he disappeared into the crowd.

Everything slowed down remarkably the second week.

The fair itself had gotten the press it was going to, so the groups of reporters, and thankfully the PR bimbi, weren't around any longer. All the important, big-time, superfantastic clients had come early to be part of all the pomp and circumstance of the first few days, and all the people who fancied themselves big-time and superfantastic but actually weren't had come over the weekend. Unless something completely out of the ordinary happened, it seemed pretty clear that two sculptures remained unsold, one of them being *Untitled #6*, the best of the very, very best, the current toast of the art world, the object of Dick's unrelenting, maniacal obsession.

The energy of the fair subsided, and down every aisle dealers and gallery employees strolled, hands behind backs, looking left and looking right, subtly discerning how many red dots indicating a sale were on the price lists of other galleries.

All the enthusiasm and excitement slipped out of me also, though I didn't mind being bored. I kind of liked it. I sat in my chair at the chrome desk and watched people walk by. I thought about how, except for a few dealers and occasional gallery girls I recognized from openings in New York, and Karina Kratsch in the next booth, I didn't really know anyone in London. There was something very lonely but also very freeing about the anonymity. Nobody knew my name, or my insecurities and fears. To them, nothing bad had ever happened to me. To strangers, it was possible I was on my way to becoming my very own superstar, just like Dick or Karina or even Ian. Then the phone rang and just like that, I wasn't anonymous anymore.

"Jane Laine! Hi! George Oreganato here. I just got into town last night! I'm manning our booth for the second week. How's it going there? What booth are you in? I'll pop over."

"B3," I told him without enthusiasm and hung up.

Boredom is so much better than George Oreganato.

Successful and supposedly a great salesperson for the Felden and Kamer Gallery in New York, George has the dubious distinction of being the only person in the world with a crush on me. He never seemed to notice that I had a boyfriend for most of the years I had known him; though he'd met Jack at openings and even on the street once, he'd never quite put two and two together. Or maybe he did and just didn't care. Neither meeting Jack nor my constant, courteous declines to invitations had ever stopped him from asking me out. And for big nights, too, like Valentine's Day and New Year's Eve, even the private party after the opening of the Fall Art Fair.

But even had there never been Jack, George Oreganato still wouldn't be for me.

He has big teeth—that bothers me—and he is way too eager beaver, always saying, "Hi! George Oreganato here!" with glad-to-meet-ya bravado. He also says "as always" way too much. He wears bow ties at the age of thirty, and argyle socks, and something about the way he's always so matchy-matchy and coordinated makes him not so much like a Ken doll in my eyes, but actually kind of like Barbie. I picture

George wrapped up in a little box with a wall of clear plastic in front of him, argyle socks peeking out from under his pants, a painting in one hand, his other outstretched, ready with a hearty handshake as "Hi! George Oreganato here!" plays out of some hidden speaker.

"Jane! How are you? Great to see you! As always, I might add," he said as he walked into my booth, bending down to kiss one cheek and then the other.

"Hi, George. Nice to see you, too."

"Well, London certainly seems to be agreeing with you. You look smashing. As always," he winked and then continued, "How's it going? How're things selling? Where're you staying? Is Ian Rhys-Fitzsimmons actually here? Is that true?"

"Thanks. Things are going well. I'm staying in the West End. Yes, Ian was here. He's gone away for a week but he'll be back on Monday. We're having an exhibition at the Sloane Gallery on Duke Street," I explained, as I'd been explaining all along, except generally, people asking about Ian didn't ask me about where I was staying or how I was doing.

"Right. Great idea: the Art Fair Project. That man's a true genius. We're doing pretty well here. Secondary market's going a bit easier than the new stuff. Have you been to the booth? You should," he went on and on, punctuating each question and comment with various winks, nods, grins, and nudges.

I was desperately thinking of what I could be busy with, so that if he asked me out I would have something to say other than, "I'd love to."

"What's going on tonight? Do you know of anything? Do you want to grab some dinner?"

"Oh, George. I'm sorry, I already have plans," I said as if I were really sorry, though I shouldn't have added the "I'm-sorry" cadence to my voice as it only invited a follow-up.

"Too bad. Well, I'm here for another ten days. Another time, then?"

"Yes, sure, I'd love to." *No, never, I don't want to.*

"When?"

Damn! "Um. I'm not exactly sure of my schedule. I need to wait and see when Ian is coming back before I can make any solid plans."

"I thought you said he was coming back on Monday?"

"I did? Um. Right, yes, but it might be earlier," I said with probably a few more *"ums"* than I am actually remembering.

"Okay, Jane, I'm sure we'll work something out," he said without any signs of discouragement. A wink, another big-toothed smile, and an invading of personal space squeeze of my shoulder, and he was gone.

And before I knew it, the week was gone, too. The first art fair of the Art Fair Project was getting ready to close its doors. As I carefully took apart masterpieces and packed up daring displays of raw genius, all according to the graph paper charts on which Ian explained every last detail about how to disassemble and pack up each sculpture, I thought how it had been a good two weeks. How with each day that I was away, I felt a little bit more like the person I used to be.

15

GIVE ME THIS ONE

"Everybody winds up kissing
the wrong person goodnight."
—Andy Warhol

Ian returned, arriving at the Sloane Gallery right on time, before the truck arrived with the disassembled sculptures, boxed up according to his graph paper. He was in high spirits and eager to help with the installation. His complexion had a ruddy flush to it as he spoke excitedly to Mr. Sloane about the beauty of the countryside, and the inspiration he had felt just walking outside. You'd think he'd been running through the moors with Heathcliff and Cathy themselves. I pictured Ian in brightly colored attire dashing across the moors, squinting through his glasses, in a desperate search for the safety of Thrushcross Grange, the genteel and much more civilized house away from the Heights where the more sane people lived. As I watched Ian gesturing enthusiastically, I made a mental note to buy a copy of *Wuthering Heights*. I thought I should definitely reread it while in London. I've always loved that book. There's something so very comforting about the fact that in the middle of God-forsaken nowhere, in the late eighteenth century, people were still absolutely, completely, fucking crazy.

We set up two new sculptures along with some of Ian's sketches, nicely framed. As we waited for the special moving truck containing *Untitled #6* to arrive, I thought about the opening and the private party being held at the Wapping Hydraulic Factory that evening. Although I often go to openings in New York, to the point that they aren't all that special anymore, I've never been invited to a post-opening private party. Dick always hosts private parties at the Lotos Club, a perfectly beautiful club on Sixty-sixth Street, right off Fifth Avenue, where I think John Singer Sargent once belonged, and where his portraits still hang. It is elegant and exclusive and charming. I only know this because one year Dick had a Christmas dinner there and I had to pass out Secret Santa gifts. It was very uncomfortable standing there all night, so much like a Christmas elf.

That unfortunate evening aside, I've never been invited to any Dick Reese Gallery private parties. Occasionally Victor will be invited, reporting back to me that the evening was beyond stuffy, totally dull, and that Dick truly needed to move his dinners to a downtown venue, Contemporary art scenesters having no home above Fifty-seventh Street. Though Mr. Sloane seemed as stuffy and pretentious as Dick, it also seemed he was a bit more in touch, a bit more clued in. The Wapping Hydraulic Factory was the coolest place in town, or so I'd been hearing all day long. The restaurant was literally inside an old power station surrounded by huge hydraulic pumps, and there were two rooms that house art exhibitions. Anyone who read art magazines would know that Ian was a member of Home House, and Soho House, and every other superexclusive superposh private club in London. I knew it, and it had crossed my mind during the downtime of the past week that somehow I would get to go to one of those places with him, and maybe see Madonna and Guy Ritchie. Jude Law might be nice also, come to think of it. But going to the Wapping Hydraulic Factory, this place that was the truest, hippest, most *right-this-very-fabulous-second* place made getting an invite to any of the private social clubs now seem like nothing at all.

The Wapping Hydraulic Factory was indeed the "nowest" place I had ever been to. I felt so pleased with myself; happy, secure, and confident in the trendy hipness. Across the room, up against a wall, I noticed Mr. Sloane. He did not look comfortable at all; he looked, in fact, as if he were in a tremendous amount of pain. He occasionally pulled it together, albeit momentarily, to wanly smile and welcome a client of his gallery. The clients and collectors were actually in much smaller numbers than the many hip London artists and their throngs of slick, chain-smoking friends, all seeming to know Ian very well, and to like him even more.

"Having a nice time?" Ian asked as he walked up to me holding two flutes of champagne. I already had my own flute in one hand and caviar on top of a little tiny potato pancake that I'd just taken off a passing tray.

"I am, yes. Thanks. And you?" I asked.

"Absolutely." Ian could pull off holding two drinks. Not everyone can. "I didn't think James would indeed go for this idea when I suggested it. I thought being home and all, with all my mates, it'd be lovely to have a party at a place I'd go to on an off night. Rather than somewhere I'd actually rather not be," he said, and then looked away from me for a minute, out at the room, genuinely happy with all the people that were there.

"Totally," I said and hoped it didn't sound as Valley Girl to Ian as it did to me. "Completely," I added, trying to sound professional, nodding my head and looking out at the room. My eyes stopped briefly again at Mr. Sloane, twitching and glancing back and forth, looking like he'd much rather be hunting grouse. It all made a lot more sense that Ian had picked the venue. Interesting, this revelation that Ian actually had off nights, that not every night was about cocktail parties and compliments. "Well then," I said and smiled. I finished my glass of champagne and put it down on a table. He offered me the other glass in his hand, and I thanked him for it.

"I'm going to get some more potato pancakes," I said, nervously. "Want some?"

He smiled at me; I smiled back and headed toward a tray-bearing waiter. I didn't make it. As I headed past the door, I took a quick look to see how many more posh friends of Ian's were walking in. As if the door had just been struck by lightning, something caught my eye. It grabbed my attention and held it. I froze where I stood, my stomach jumping up, flipping over, flipping back and jumping down. *What is he doing here? Does he know Ian? Does it really matter why he's here? Does anything at all really matter other than the fact that he is here?* I couldn't do anything but stand in one place and stare at him, vision of perfection that he is; I was amazed I didn't just dribble to the floor. Tall doesn't begin to explain him. Gorgeous could never do him justice. Beautiful is ugly when standing next to him. There are no words complimentary enough, or anything enough, to describe him. Well, that's not entirely true. It's not like there are no words at all, because in fact there are two:

Owen. Wilson.

Owen Wilson was walking into the same restaurant that I was in. In about a second and a half, Owen Wilson was going to be in the same room I was in. I was going to be in the same room Owen Wilson was in! Perfect body, perfect hair, perfect eyes, and completely perfect nose. I wanted to get closer; I wanted to hear his perfect voice. But still I was unable to move. I saw him nodding at a couple of people and I saw him shake hands with someone. He started walking in my direction. Maybe he was going to walk right up to me, tip his cowboy hat—he wasn't actually wearing a cowboy hat, but maybe he could get one somewhere between the door and where I was standing—look into my eyes and say, "I wanna be a cowboy, baby." I'd smile and look sexy and flip my hair around and as I put my arms around his neck, he'd put each of his hands on either side of my waist and pull me toward him really quickly. I'd look deeply into his beautiful eyes and tell him, "I wanna be your cowgirl."

"Jane! Hi! Hi there! Come on over, I've got two clients you should meet. They're interested in Ian's work and asked who was here from Dick Reese Gallery. You look beautiful tonight, as always."

What? Owen Wilson is no longer in my line of vision. All I can see are teeth!

"Jane? Are you okay? Do you need some water? You look kinda weird."

Why in my mind did I hear Owen Wilson saying, "I wanna be a cowboy, baby," when what I actually saw was George Oreganato telling me I looked kinda weird? Why was what happened in my mind always so different from what happened in the real world?

"No, thanks, George. I'm fine. How are you?" I asked, trying to look around him.

"Great! Great! Do you want to meet those clients?"

I really, really don't. "Yes, sure," I answered, somewhat dazed, and followed George to a table where we joined a couple.

"He really is a very special artist," I said in response to their exclamations about Ian and his work. George stayed at the table with us, so if any sale resulted from the conversation his gallery would get a cut. Also he stayed there just so he could bother me. As always. The clients said they'd come by the gallery during the next week to have another look. They seemed very happy and pleased as we all started to get up. Then, fantastically, amazingly, there was Owen Wilson again! *Hi Owen!* He sat down at a table in front of us. Owen was facing in and I was facing in so we were *facing each other!* I sat down again as quickly as I could, transfixed. George stayed next to me and kept talking but I couldn't hear him. I couldn't hear anything except Owen Wilson's voice at the end of *Bottle Rocket,* when he looked at Luke Wilson and said, "Give me this one. Give me this one. Ya gotta give me this one." It was almost as if I were hearing my own voice pleading with Cupid. *Give me this one. Give me this one. Ya gotta give me this one.* He was slouched down in his chair with his long legs stretched out. Then he looked at me.

OWEN WILSON AND I MADE EYE CONTACT!

I looked away, scared; I couldn't handle it. When I got the nerve to look back again, Owen Wilson smiled at me. This time I didn't get scared; I didn't look away. I remembered a million years ago when I first met Jack and I had thought that the gods had smiled on me and that fate was my friend; that everything that had ever happened had happened so that I would meet Jack. I was wrong about all of that. That time. Because *this* time I was right. This time I'd arrived, without any baggage—actually with some baggage, with quite a lot even—at the doorstep of The Perfect Man.

Maybe this was my one opportunity. Maybe this was my one chance.

I couldn't let it pass me by. I had to take it!

I was going to get up from the table and walk up to Owen Wilson and say to him, for real, not just in my head, "I wanna be a cowgirl, baby." Well, maybe I could just say "Hi. I'm Jane Laine." I had nothing at all to lose. And if this really was my one opportunity, then how could I not seize it? How could I let him walk out of my life as quickly as he had walked in, to meet someone else, fall in love with her, and marry her, leaving me to know, for the rest of my life, that it should have been me?

I took a really deep breath, finished what was left of my champagne, stood up, and started walking the short distance to where Owen Oh My God Wilson sat.

"Jane! Wait!" exclaimed George, jumping up from his seat.

But I couldn't wait, I couldn't wait for George. I knew what I had to do and nothing, not anything was going to stop me. Except George had somehow gotten directly in my path, and had, quite literally, stopped me. He put his hands on my shoulders and for a horrible second I thought he was about to shake me.

"George. Really, look, I'm sorry but I have to go."

"Jane, haven't you listened to *anything* I've said?"

Actually I hadn't. "George. Can't we talk about this later? There's something I really nee—"

"Jane," he said urgently as he tightened his grip on my shoulders, "I mean it. Don't you see how much I like you? How much I've always liked you?"

Before I could even think, "What?" or "Ew" or "Oh no" or "Not now," it was all teeth and hair and bow tie and collision and then George Oreganato was kissing me. I pulled away as quickly as I could, which, as it turned out, was too quickly; all I saw was argyle as I collided with the floor.

"Oh, Jane, I'm so sorry, are you okay?"

George bent down and I felt bad about pulling away so ungracefully that it seemed I was repulsed. I didn't want to kiss George but I didn't want to make him feel bad either. "I'm fine, I, uh. I have to go!" I said, jumping up and hoping Owen hadn't seen the kiss and subsequent fall. I looked over to where he had been, only to see he wasn't there anymore. I looked around. Owen Wilson wasn't anywhere.

Owen Wilson was gone.

The night was close to over and Ian and Mr. Sloane weren't around, so hopefully they hadn't seen any of the tragic display. I got my coat and umbrella and walked slowly out into the street. I didn't put my umbrella up, though. Instead I walked alone in the rain. *I probably would have spazzed out anyway,* I told myself, *and not had anything to say after "I'm Jane."* Owen Wilson could have had any woman in the entire world, so chances were he probably wouldn't want me.

It didn't help; nothing could stop me from believing that I might very well spend the remainder of my days much in the same way as I'd spent so many days before: kissing the wrong guy.

16

WHERE ARE MY SURFACES?

"I am a deeply superficial person."

—Andy Warhol

The Sloane Gallery is a lot brighter than the Dick Reese Gallery, and the St. James area of London is prettier and far more elegant than the Chelsea area of New York is. I was given my own desk and a computer. Mr. Sloane did his part to make me feel at home by terrorizing his staff so they hurried around dancing on eggshells, hardly speaking to each other and not ever speaking to me. When clients came into the gallery to see Ian's sculptures, the woman at the front desk would watch me, wait until a few preliminary questions had been answered, and then buzz for Mr. Sloane. He would appear scowling, then smile at the clients and ask how he could help them.

Ian often came to my desk, asking for a checklist or relaying a story. He even came over once or twice to eat his lunch with me. One day I asked him if he liked something, and he smiled this very big smile and said he *really*, really did. My initial reaction was, "Back off with my expression, buddy," but he looked so pleased with himself I left it alone.

The days sped by in the afternoons, when I could e-mail to New York and Miami and get immediate responses. Kate was busy with Diego and their daughter, and thrilled I was having a nice time. Victor said he missed me madly, and that Dick was a raving lunatic about the unsold status of *Untitled #6*. Elizabeth wanted to know where I'd be in mid-December. She thought Chicago but wanted to be sure, so she could have my bridesmaid dress sent there, so it could be altered in time for her wedding. I knew I was missing all of Elizabeth's pre-wedding festivities. All of the lingerie showers, and the kitchen showers, and truthfully, I didn't mind. I've always thought the shower thing is all backward—why can't there be showers for people who might never get married? Aren't they, in fact, in much more need of gifts? I e-mailed my Chicago hotel information to her and confirmed my measurements, lying about actually getting out a measuring tape and double-checking. I was probably the worst bridesmaid ever. As I sent Elizabeth's e-mail off, one arrived from George—never-to-be-forgiven George—asking about New Year's Eve.

Ian left again at the end of the week, off to Yorkshire, off to the moors, leaving me without lunch visits. On his last day in the gallery, we had a cocktail party. An Ian-is-leaving-so-please-come-and-have-a-cheese-stick party. As I ate one, and drank another glass of champagne, I wondered how many glasses of champagne had been consumed throughout the world in honor of Ian Rhys-Fitzsimmons and his work? I turned then to look at *Untitled #6,* and looking at it suddenly made everything feel a little bit warmer, like everything was all for some purpose.

When I got back to my hotel that night I logged on to Hotmail and there, shining like a beacon, was another e-mail from Victor.

Mail to: "Victor's Party List"

From: Victor@DickReeseGallery.com

Re: The Second Most Wonderful Night of the Year

MISS USA'S ON TOMORROW NIGHT!!!

You all know the drill. Come over between 8:15 and 8:30—don't think of arriving during the show. I will: clean obsessively, order too much food for a bunch of people who don't eat, be inappropriately drunk at 8:45 and start throwing out phrases like "lack of facial symmetry" and "baby got back" too loudly soon afterward. Bring nothing; invite whomever you'd like (so long as we don't have to justify ourselves or explain why judging people based solely on appearance is fun). Don't worry about RSVPing, and wear something normal (you're wrong if you think "nobody's" ever showed up in drag or in a tiara before—you'll only feel stupid for doing so later).—VH

An overwhelming homesickness moved in. I had almost forgotten the things in New York that made me happy. I missed going to parties where I knew all the people. I missed parties that happened just because people wanted to see their friends, not because an art fair was opening. I clicked around on my fancy television looking for something American, but became distracted by *Absolutely Fabulous*. Edina was trying to clean up her house because very neat friends were coming to visit. She was running around trying to straighten up, all the while asking, "Surfaces, darling, surfaces? Where are my surfaces?" I pictured Dick running around, clapping his hands saying, "Neat and clean, neat and clean. I want this booth neat and clean. Right! Now!" That sucked the fun out of *Absolutely Fabulous,* so I turned it off. It was 10:30 in London, which meant 5:30 in New York which was perfect because, it being Friday, Dick would be in Fire Island, hopefully freezing in the off-season. Victor would just be getting ready to leave. I dialed quickly, double-hoping I would catch him.

"DICK REESE GALLERY!"

"Hi, Clarissa, it's Jane. How are you?"

There was only silence on the other end of the phone.

"Clarissa?"

"Ye-es?" She was completely, utterly confused.

"Hi. It's Jane Laine."

"Oooooh. YES! JANE! Hi!"

Was I *that* easily forgettable? After only three weeks and two days? Maybe Clarissa thought I had been fired? Whenever fired people call about their COBRA health care plans, or their severance check, Clarissa acts like she never knew them. Had I been fired? Even with the vast knowledge I had accumulated about the evil that is Dick, I couldn't quite believe he had fired me and hadn't filled me in. "Um, hi. Is Victor there, Clarissa?"

"HOLD PLEASE!"

"Jane Laine. As I live and breathe! You won't believe this, but I was just kicking back here at the old desk, waiting for the double agent Velociraptor to leave to give you a call and have a nice long talk on the Dick Reese dime."

"Beat ya to it! Hi!"

"How are you, honey?"

"Victor, I'm great, but I have to ask you something first. Have I been fired that you know of?"

"What? No! Are you crazy? You haven't been fired."

"Okay, good. No, not crazy, swear. How aaarrrre you?

"Oh, just fabulous, *fabulous*. Having my Miss USA Party tomorrow and going to Man Ray tonight with a dealer from Gagosian. H-O-T. Hot. We'll talk a little business and then expense it. Oh, I'm so naughty but it's the only way I can deal with the pain of working for Dick without you here."

"Right, Victor." Dick is always nice to Victor, Victor being handsome and charming and Dick being lecherous and creepy. "I miss you."

"I miss you, too. But there isn't anything new with me. It's the same, just me and all the girls in Chelsea. Tell me about you, that's what I want to hear."

"Well, you aren't going to believe this, but with the exception of getting very homesick when I read your e-mail, I actually like it here. It is so much easier knowing that there is an ocean between Dick and me, and being in charge has been good. Things are good."

"I knew it. You so deserve it. And see, Ian's nice, right?" he asked.

"Yeah," I confessed, "Ian's fine actually." Even as I said it, I worried about Ian being fine. If Ian was indeed fine, was indeed nice, then maybe he wasn't the fraud I had all along suspected him to be. I didn't want to think that, though. I couldn't think that. Because if Ian wasn't the fraud . . . who was?

"Do you hang out with him at all?" Victor asked, mercifully taking me away from my thoughts. "Jane, think about it—you're in London with *Ian Rhys-Fitzsimmons*. When you forget about Dick, that's pretty fucking awesome."

"I know, it kind of is."

"Go anywhere supercool?" he asked.

"The party after the opening was at this restaurant in a hydraulic factory that was the coolest supercool place I've ever been. Victor, it was amazing. And— Oh! God! You'll never guess who I saw!"

"Who?"

"Guess!"

"David Duchovny?"

"Better!"

"Who's better than David Duchovny?

"Okay, maybe not better to you, but also not married to Téa Leoni."

"No!"

"Yes!"

"You better not be lying!"

"I'm not!"

"Owen Fucking Wilson?"

"Owen Wilson."

"Oh my God! Oh. My. God. Tell me everything."

Victor listened to every last detail of the Owen Wilson sighting, right down to its dismal final moments. Like the perfect friend he was, he vowed to always and forever send death rays in George Oreganato's direction, and did his best to convince me it might not be the last time I'd ever see Owen. I wanted to believe him. We talked for a little while longer and actually, it turned out that Victor did have some news of his own. He'd had a run-in with the one guy he ever really loved, the one guy who really broke his heart. It wasn't an actual run-in with the heartbreaker himself, but with a very good friend of his. It's actually much better that way, Victor explained, because seeing the friend of the person who stepped on your heart isn't going to kill you all over again, the way it could if you saw the actual heartbreaker. Seeing the friend, you can maintain an air of fabulousness, of composure, of "I am so over your pointless, little, little friend and please go tell him how great I look."

And Victor, lucky, perfect Victor had gotten to do just that.

He'd been with some superstunning friend who wisely put all the connections together and lovingly held Victor's hand and stroked his back and acted like the most devoted boyfriend ever. Victor told The Heartbreaker's friend how great everything was and never once asked about the guy who broke his heart, the equivalent of a loudspeaker blaring, "I am so over all of it."

"And you know, it was nice to see him," Victor added. "He's doing really well. He and his partner just adopted a baby from China. I think that's amazing."

"I think it's amazing, too. I *really,* really hope that one day I can do that," I told Victor wistfully.

"Really, Jane?"

"Oh, of course."

"Good for you! I never saw you as the type to adopt from another country. That's so admirable. It absolutely is."

"Thanks," I said, a little too quickly. "Okay, well, I should get to sleep. It was heaven talking to you, Victor. Let's do it again soon."

"Real soon. Love you."

"Love you, too."

I felt ashamed as I hung up because I'd lied. I didn't have a tremendous interest in adopting a Chinese baby. What I had *meant* was I hoped I would run into a friend of Jack's one day, with a really gorgeous guy standing right next to me.

17

WAIT!

"I always wish I had died. I still wish that because I could have gotten the whole thing over with."
—Andy Warhol

On our last day at the Sloane Gallery, as I focused on getting everything packed up and ready to fly to the next fair, I was hoping Rome would be as good as London. When Ian arrived, in jeans, a bright pink, green, and purple plaid shirt, a navy blazer, and some sort of desert boot–like shoe, I didn't think he looked ridiculous. To me he looked cool. *Maybe it's his blazer,* I thought. *I've always had a weakness for a man who wears a blazer.*

The packing went smoothly. Ian helped place the sculptures into their crates while Mr. Sloane appeared intermittently to order members of his staff around. I packed up anything that was left of our paperwork and checked our e-mails (nothing exciting). *Untitled #6* was the last thing to be packed, as it was traveling to the airport in its own special truck and being packed by two special movers. Although still unsold, the sculpture was now a media star. This was perfectly fitting for a creation of Ian's.

The special movers, two young Indian men, arrived at the gallery at four P.M., leaving us all exactly two hours, more than enough time, to get the sculpture safely packed away, snugly protected and ready to travel to the airport. As the two men wheeled the transport apparatus up to the sculpture, they talked hurriedly and animatedly. If Dick had been there, the sight would have had him marching around, clapping his hands, demanding that no one speak as they handled a Rhys-Fitzsimmons sculpture. The men kept talking as they prepared to transfer the sculpture from the gallery floor to the wheeled platform. I looked over at Ian, thinking briefly that I might see him getting ready to clap. He was on the other side of the room packing a removable piece from a smaller sculpture. So he didn't see the first slip, the first misstep in motion that I saw. It wasn't until I yelled, "WAIT!" that he knew something was wrong.

Untitled #6 was at an angle, tipping. It was impossible to think that it might be falling. "WAIT!" I yelled. It may have seemed I was yelling at the men, but as I watched *Untitled #6* arching toward the floor, it was the sculpture I was yelling at. Maybe I thought I could influence it by talking to it; maybe I thought I could stop it from falling? So Ian wouldn't self-destruct, and Dick wouldn't kill me in retribution for the many, many hundreds of thousands of dollars he would lose?

Pain knifed through me as one part of the sculpture scraped

down the wall and then gouged into the wood floor. Then the bottom part buckled, unable to support its own weight, and collapsed. It happened quickly but as if in slow motion.

With much banging and scraping, *Untitled #6* became unrecognizable.

It was now only pieces of steel lying on a scraped and dented floor.

I stood there with my hand over my mouth. I was looking at wreckage that had been the greatest contribution to twenty-first-century art only a few moments earlier. I looked over at Ian, waiting for the explosion that was bound to come, waiting for crisp, properly pronounced expletives. The two deliverymen stood frozen, looking from me to Ian to Mr. Sloane, clearly waiting, in the same way I was, for someone to start yelling and screaming and cursing and threatening.

Ian stood frozen for what seemed like an eternity.

Then one of the men broke the silence, yelling apologies in his own language. The more frantically he wailed, the more scared he looked, and the more worried I got that he was going to cry. The other man didn't look much better. Forgetting for a moment about Ian and his sculpture, I felt so bad for the two men. Even though they had been careless, they both seemed so distraught I wished I could fast-forward to the part where it would all be my fault, so I wouldn't have to watch them be blamed and yelled at and fired.

"It's okay," Ian said to the two men, to everyone in the gallery.

Then he got up and walked across the gallery floor, stepping over the remains of his masterpiece without really looking at it. He walked over to the more upset of the two men and reassuringly rested a hand on his shoulder. "It's okay. Really. I know you didn't do this on purpose. Accidents happen. I know that they do," he said softly.

Mr. Sloane, red in the face, started navigating his way through the remains of the sculpture with short, angry steps, intermittently looking down, then up with an expression of unmitigated disgust.

"It's okay," Ian told him, and the calmness and authority in his voice seemed to drain the angry color from Sloane's face. Still, he was obviously enraged at the loss of the sculpture, and at the damage to his gallery. He asked Ian, in escalating decibels, "Wasn't this going to be the pivotal part of your exhibition in Rome? Wasn't this your greatest artistic achievement to date?"

"Well, James," Ian said without sarcasm or irony, "it appears that isn't any longer the case."

Steady and collected, Ian coolly went about asking the men if they were up to packing the fragments in a separate crate. He quietly explained to Mr. Sloane that he would send the pieces back to his studio in New York and deal with disposing of them there. He looked at the various art handlers and gallery staff who had assembled, then smiled and said softly that they were only pieces of steel and repeated that it was okay.

I wanted to hug Ian right then. I wanted to tell him I admired him for his calm and for being more concerned with people than with sculpture. After spending years watching Dick Reese fly off the handle at the drop of a hat, let alone the drop of a sculpture, I had forgotten it was actually possible to deal with a crisis like a normal human being. As I watched Ian diffuse the anxiety without even raising his voice,

I realized it was entirely possible that he might be the only normal person in a position of power in the art world that I had ever encountered.

I had to call Dick to tell him what had happened.

I would rather have been under the sculpture as it fell than have the conversation I was going to have. I figured Ian would want to talk to Dick after I did; I hoped maybe he would want to talk to Dick *instead* of me. I went to find him to let him know I was calling. After looking through the gallery, I walked outside to the delivery truck that held the pieces of the sculpture. It was dark outside, windy and rainy.

I saw Ian in profile, staring blankly into the truck. I didn't walk up to him, I just stood under the awning of the gallery and waited. There was something so private and sad about the way he was standing, I thought of walking back inside. Yet with the rain coming sideways underneath the awning, with the shelter and safety of the gallery behind me, I felt that of all the wrong things I'd ever done, the most wrong thing would be to go back inside. After a few moments I walked slowly over and stood next to Ian. I looked into the truck at the crate holding the twisted, broken pieces. He didn't say anything, but he took off his blazer and put it over my shoulders. I wished I had something, anything, I could give to him to let him know somehow it would be okay.

I reached over and took his hand. For a long time, we stood there, holding hands and staring into the back of that van with the rain pouring down on us. And even though it was so cold, the fact that he held onto my hand made me feel warmer than I could remember feeling before. When he turned again to look at me, for a second I was sure I couldn't breathe.

"Thank you, Jane," he said in a whisper.

"Thanks," I said and even though "Thanks" clearly wasn't the most logical thing to say right then, in a way it made sense.

I headed back to the gallery, but before I went in I turned around. He had lifted his right hand to his face and I realized he wasn't wiping at rain; he was wiping away tears. I hurried back inside.

I sat at the empty desk and watched one of the art handlers measure the gouge in the floor. Tomorrow, repairs would be made and a new exhibition would be starting. Tomorrow, as quickly as it had arrived, *Ian Rhys-Fitzsimmons: Art Fair Project* would be gone. I wondered if any of the successes of the past month would count, or if the only thing London would be was the place where Ian's greatest work had been destroyed.

All the things I had said and thought about Ian spun through my head.

I remembered the times I had called him stupid, annoying, a smarty-pants and a know-it-all. I remembered all the times when rather than listen to what he had to say, I would repeat *blah blah blah* in my mind. I'd called him ridiculous. I'd imagined he was secretly from some scary part of Idaho. I'd thought again and again that he was a fraud and a fake. I couldn't remember if I had ever called him an idiot, but I knew with complete certainty that *I* was one.

I was the idiot. *I* was the fraud. *I* was the fake. Not Ian. *Me*.

Why had I been so sure he didn't really care about what he was doing? I had been completely, utterly wrong about

Ian. He walked into the gallery and came over to the desk where I was sitting. I hoped he never knew all the things I had thought about him. I said I was going to call Dick, and asked if he wanted to talk to him. He shook his head and asked if I could just fill him in.

"Sure, Ian. I'll let him know. And I'm sorry, I really am."

He put his hands in his pockets and looked down. "Thanks, Jane." Then, slowly, he pushed his foot in an arc across a small area of the floor. "Are you all right getting back to the hotel?" he asked, focusing everything on his foot as it traveled back and forth.

"I'm fine," I told him. "I just have to make this call and then I'll head back."

"Well then. Cheers, Jane. I'll see you in the morning."

With his hands still in his pockets, and his head still down, he turned around and began walking across the gallery toward the door. Then he stopped. Afraid he would turn and see that I had been watching him leave, I grabbed the phone and took a deep breath as I dialed New York, and then another as I listened to it ringing. I heard the gallery door shut behind Ian, and only then realized I hadn't said anything after he said good-bye.

Cheers, Ian, I thought to myself. *See you in the morning.*

"DICK REESE GALLERY!"

I took one more breath, hoped it wouldn't be my last, and asked to speak to Dick.

18

GRAPH PAPER DRAWING #1

"An artist is someone who produces things
that people don't need to have but that
he—for some reason—thinks it would be
a good idea to give them."
—Andy Warhol

The next morning, Ian picked me up at 5 Maddox and we headed back to Heathrow Airport. There was no, "Cheers, Jane," when I got in the car. Ian looked quietly out his window, and I worried his spirit had been broken right along with *Untitled #6*. I looked out my own window, at the billboard ads that once seemed so foreign and now so familiar. As raindrops raced across the window, it seemed a lifetime had passed since the last time we'd been on our way to the airport. I turned to Ian to say as much, but stopped when I saw his sad expression. I wanted to tell him I knew what it felt like to worry you'd feel empty for all the rest of the days in front of you.

Ian carried my bags to the curb and paid the driver even though I was supposed to do that with Dick Reese money. He loaded my bags, right next to his, onto one of the airport carts and we walked slowly, him pushing, up to the check-in counter.

"Good morning," an efficient-sounding voice said. For a moment I thought I'd miss hearing English accents, then realized that eventually Ian would speak again so I'd hear an English accent no matter where I was.

"Good morning," I answered handing over our tickets and my passport. Ian handed his over, too, nodding in acknowledgment that it was morning, although he didn't seem ready to say there was anything good about it.

"All right then, Jane Laine," check-in man said, and looked briefly at me, "has anyone given you anything to bring on the plane?"

"No."

"Have you been in possession of your bags since you packed them?"

"Yes."

"Right then. You are in seat 2B. Your flight will start boarding in an hour," he informed me and turned his attention to Ian. "Ian Rhys-Fitzsimmons?" he said, a subtle flash of recognition in his eyes, and then began asking the same questions.

I was mesmerized, looking at my ticket. It had a big red "Upgrade" stamp on it, and my seat assignment was in first class. First class? *Has there been a mixup?* I looked up to ask and heard, "Splendid. Your seat is 2A."

"Thank you," said Ian, retrieving his ticket and passport. *How had this happened? Had Amanda made a mistake that resulted in my good fortune?* I doubted it. Then I knew. My seat assignment had nothing to do with Amanda.

"Thank you," I said to Ian as we walked toward our gate.

"What for?" he asked. Then he smiled, the first I'd seen all morning. I felt my spirits lift. I smiled back and didn't say anything else, and he didn't seem to mind.

We both got to wait for our flight in the special private lounge available only to business and first-class travelers. There were lots of free bottles of water and free fruit. I imagined it was probably not important to stock up; the flight attendants in first class probably give you water whenever you ask for it, and fruit, too, but still. I couldn't stop myself from gathering water and an apple and a banana. I asked Ian if he wanted anything, but he didn't. He was looking out the window, not talking, not smiling, not writing in his journals or on his graph paper. I noticed that his hair was standing up on one side of his head. I told him I wanted to go buy some magazines, and he nodded absently.

I picked up the November issue of *Art Forum,* and then went to the celebrity and fashion section. I got *British Vogue* and instead of my normal staple, *People,* I opted instead for *Hello!* magazine, a new vice. I rationalized that although these choices were on the less intellectual side, at least they were international. I walked back to the special lounge and started to arrange my magazines so that *Art Forum,* the one that I would read last, was on top. But then I thought about Ian, and how I'd always thought he was fake and how he'd turned out to be so very real. I thought about how I'd realized yesterday that if anyone was a fake, it was, very likely me. I decided then that it was okay to read *People,* and *Hello!,* and even the occasional *Entertainment Weekly* if that was what I wanted to read. I arranged my magazines in the order I would read them.

Once we boarded, Ian and I settled into big spacious seats. Right away, I got my movie screen out of the arm and looked through the plane magazine for the list of movies. Disappointed, I learned that the flight was too short to have a movie. "Oh," I said, closing the magazine. "I guess there isn't any movie since the flight is only an hour and a half long."

"An hour and a half?" Ian asked, looking puzzled. He leaned forward and took his ticket out of his jacket to look at it. Relief washed over his features. "No, two and a half hours. See?" He handed his ticket to me. "There's a one-hour time change," he explained. "Rome's an hour ahead of London," he said, leaning back in his seat, looking more relaxed.

In that moment I wasn't sure I'd ever not think of Ian as a bit weird.

Who is happy because they'll be on a plane for an hour longer? Who wants to stay on a plane longer? I looked over at him and he was smiling and his eyes were brighter, and he was looking around the plane, noticing everything, taking everything in. He turned to me enthusiastically and started telling me about a book he'd just read. A bit later I looked out the window and noticed we were off the ground. I'd missed takeoff, and all its nerve-wrenching anxiety. I'd never missed takeoff before.

Then Ian took his graph paper out and began to sketch one of his diagrams. I really did want to understand what he was talking about this time. I looked from the graph paper to him and listened. His renewed enthusiasm was electrifying the air between us, and as he pointed with his pen at two crossing lines, looking up at me to see if I was following, it seemed everything that had happened with *Untitled* #6 had happened years ago. I wanted to be just like Ian right then. I wanted to be zealous and enthusiastic and able to get over disappointment as quickly as I was able to get all wrapped up in something new.

"How do you do it?" I asked, wanting to know so badly I didn't realize I'd voiced the question. It halted the movement of Ian's pen, and caused him to look at me.

"What's that?"

"How is everything all better? How are you okay? Didn't it break your heart yesterday? Didn't it make you want to die? How are you happy again, so fast?" I asked quickly. Maybe I shouldn't have reminded him of everything that happened, but I couldn't help myself; I needed to know. Right before he started to answer, it dawned on me whom I was asking. If anyone could truly answer my questions, it could very possibly be Ian.

"Isn't it clear, Jane? Isn't it quite obvious?" he asked me.

"Isn't what obvious?"

I could see by the way his eyes lit up that he was thinking of something great. I couldn't wait to hear what it was. But then, just as quickly, his forehead wrinkled and he seemed to be thinking of something else, something not nearly so great at all.

"Ah," he said and now I saw sadness in his eyes. "I wouldn't necessarily use the words 'all better' to describe the state of things. But, yes, you're right. I do feel like my heart has been broken. I don't think I wanted to die—think of all I'd miss out on—but I did feel pretty awful. It's not that it's over, and it's not that I've forgotten." He paused, looked out the window, and then turned back to me. "It's just that there isn't anything I can do about it, and I have other things that give me happiness. The only thing to do is to concentrate on those things and accept the loss, terrible as it was."

I wanted more, an easier solution, more of a revelation. Weren't you supposed to expect a revelation when you asked a genius to answer your questions? I went over everything he said in my mind. I thought about his having other things to be happy about and wondered what they were. I thought about how he was able to accept his loss, and I didn't doubt this ability had more than a little to do with his immense success. He took off his glasses then, and rubbed his eyes. He looked like a little kid with his eyes all puffy and his hair standing up all over the place.

"Are you tired, Jane?" he asked, and I wondered how long I'd been staring.

"What? Oh, yeah, well maybe a little. Are you?"

"Yes, actually. Actually I am a bit knackered." *Knackered. Love that.* "Here," he said as he handed me the graph paper he'd been working on. "Why don't you hold on to this? A reminder that not many things in the world are so good or so bad that you can't leave them behind and continue on."

"Thanks," I said, taking the drawing. I smoothed it out, tucked it away in one of my binders, and knew I'd keep it forever. Not because his graph paper drawings were finding a market of their own, being framed and sold alongside his sculptures, and not just because I wanted to own anything by the great Ian Rhys-Fitzsimmons. I knew I would keep it always because he had given it to me on the day I first knew that he and I were going to be friends.

19

HELLO, LUCÍA

"I have no memory. Every day is a new day
because I don't remember the day before."
—Andy Warhol

Arte Contemporaneo
Rome, Italy

Mail to: planejane6@hotmail.com
From: Amanda@DickReeseGallery.com

Hello Jane,
I truly hope that everything is going well for you and Mr. Rhys-Fitzsimmons and I must say I am terribly sorry to hear about the disaster. I decided to e-mail you rather than leave you a message to be sure you are in receipt of the following important information immediately:

In light of everything that happened, Dick is on his way to Rome. He will be arriving shortly. He will be staying at the Hassler in the room reserved for you. Please let them know that the room should be switched to the name Reese. As Dick was concerned, understandably, about the added expense of three hotel rooms in Rome, I did some research via the Internet on alternate, more reasonably priced accommodations for you. After some investigating (just call me Sherlock! ☺), I discovered a great service that rents out apartments for long-term stays. One month indeed counts as long term!

After you have carefully situated Ian in his room and **switched the name of your hotel room to Reese,** you should go to the following address in Trastevere, an area very close to the center of Rome: Via Garibaldi 5, Rome 00168. The code for the gate is 3465 and your apartment number is 12.

With fondest regards, Amanda

P.S. This apartment comes with a cat. How fun for you! Instructions for her care will be on the table when you arrive.
P.P.S. Just a reminder to CHANGE THE NAME OF YOUR HOTEL ROOM TO REESE. Dick absolutely doesn't want any confusion upon his arrival.

Strangely enough, I didn't unpack my laptop in the airport, hook it up, and check my personal e-mail. Ignorance, they say, is bliss. After arriving at the hotel with Ian, unpacking everything right down to my toiletries, sending a dress to the hotel dry cleaner, enjoying a snack from the minibar, I took an hour-long nap. When I woke up, I took a long shower, using the hotel room robe and slippers. Then I left to begin setting up for our exhibition at the *Arte Contemporaneo* fair, which was being held at *Il Centro Nazionale per le Arti Contemporanee—Museo del XXI Secolo,* also known as Rome's National Center for Contemporary Arts—Museum of the Twenty-First Century.

Setting up three large sculptures in the large, hangarlike space, a former army barracks, the only worry in my mind was that there should be four sculptures instead of a trio. The only tension I felt as I shadowed the deliverymen like a lunatic was that the fate that befell #6 wouldn't befall anything else. I did not know that as I was going about my day, Dick was apoplectic in the lobby of the Hassler hotel screaming, "DO YOU HAVE ANY IDEA WHO I AM?" Or that he continued screaming it louder and louder, until he was let into the room even though it was listed under Laine, not Reese. Once inside, he was welcomed by an unmade bed, an empty Toblerone box, two empty bottles of water on the night table, and a damp bathrobe left on a chair.

I didn't hear the call he made to New York.

The call during which Amanda assured him that yes, she had indeed asked me *several* times to change the room arrangements and that yes, she was *absolutely sure* I knew to go to the apartment in Trastevere. I knew nothing about any of it at all, until I heard the screeching.

"Neat and clean! Neat AND CLEAN! I WANT THIS NEAT AND CLEAN!" Even had I not heard the quick double clap-clap that followed each screech of "neat" and of "clean," I would have been sure. Like a knife through my heart, I knew. Dick Reese was in Rome.

In one long paragraph he hurled a viperous stream of words at me—he was a fat, snapping turtle, shaking with rage. I'd lulled myself into complacency thinking I wouldn't see him until January, yet here he was. I made a mental note to remember never to get too comfortable. As I'd learned the hard way, and really should have remembered, everything, anything, can change the second you turn your back. Sometimes even if you don't.

Despite my shock and despair, I miraculously gleaned several pieces of information from the sounds Dick's forked tongue was spewing. The booth was a mess. He wanted it neat (clap-clap) and clean (clap-clap). The fact that we were unpacking was no reason for unseemly *packing materials* and *crates* to be offending him with their presence. Also, he was tired. Further, he'd been in my hotel room, though he kept referring to it as *his* hotel room, which was odd. Finally, he wanted me, no *needed* me to go right now, remove my mess, and take it to somewhere called Trastevere.

That didn't make much sense but I heard "Amanda-e-mail" several times.

With any luck I would be able to piece together the last bits of the horrid puzzle if I checked my e-mail. I looked for Ian. He wasn't anywhere around. I looked at the unpacking and the half-assembled sculptures. I'd have to get back to them later. Finishing before going back to the hotel was, without question, not an option.

I grabbed my laptop, hoping that in it there actually would be this e-mail from Amanda that would answer all the questions I had. I walked outside as quickly as I could, fighting the urge to break into a run.

The Eternal City's cutting-edge center for contemporary art is designed to create a very modern feeling right in the middle of ancient and timeless Rome. But it isn't *in* the middle of Rome. It is about half an hour north, in an area called Flaminia. I'd come here earlier with Ian, chauffeured in a hotel car, and now I had no idea how to call a taxi so I could get back to the hotel. The rumored shuttle service the fair was running between Flaminia and the city wasn't anywhere around. But then, in the distance, I saw a bus. It said Piazza del Popolo. That sounded like something that would be in Rome. If I could just get myself into the city I could ask people to point me in the direction of the Spanish Steps—that's where the hotel was. It wasn't a great plan, but I was alarmingly close to frantic and I absolutely had to get out of there.

When you get on a bus in New York without money, you don't get past the driver. In Rome, however, doors open up at the back of the bus, so you don't have to go past the driver at all if you don't want to. I didn't have any Italian change yet, didn't have any sort of ticket, and didn't know the rules of how you were supposed to pay. Since the only thing I knew how to say in Italian was, *"Dov' e?,"* meaning "where is?," I simply got on the back of the bus and sat down as quickly as I could.

I didn't want to scam a free Italian bus ride. I simply could NOT go back in and tell Dick I didn't know how to get back into Rome. Sometimes you have to do things you don't want to do. *That* I learned a long time ago.

And I learned some new things after I got on the bus. I learned that to ride a bus in Rome, you need a ticket that you must stamp in a stamping machine once you get on said bus.

If you don't have a stamped ticket, when an official-looking man gets on the bus and asks to see your stamped ticket, you get charged *cinquante euro*.

"*Dov' e?*" I asked several times.

"*No biglietta! Cinquante euro, Signorina!*" he said back, really more times than I thought necessary.

Finally a bilingual person on the bus explained that *cinquante euro* was fifty euros, about fifty dollars. So I paid fifty dollars for a trip that should have cost about a dollar, and made my way to the Piazza del Popolo. And thankfully, Piazza del Popolo wasn't off on a hilltop in the middle of some serene Tuscan town. It was in a beautiful, busy, possibly central, part of Rome.

"*Dov' e* taxi?"

I managed to "*dov' e*" myself to a white sign with Taxi written on it, and a line of white cars underneath. I got into a cab and tried to act like I wasn't a tourist, so the driver wouldn't take me totally out of my way on some scenic tour. "Hassler," I said, hoping it would be enough. Luckily it did the trick.

As I got out of the taxi, exhausted, hot and sweaty and stressed out, in front of my beautiful hotel, right atop the breathtaking expanse of the Spanish Steps, all I could think about was one thing. Dick had seen my bras and all my underwear. I had left them out on the desk. He'd never know, not in a million years, that women wore thong underwear so they didn't have panty lines, not because secretly they were porn stars.

As soon as I entered the lobby, I plugged in my laptop, downloaded my e-mail, and read Amanda's, the one with the little red high-priority exclamation point next to it. Damning it to hell, right along with its sender, I charged up to the room—*Dick's* room—and packed everything as quickly as I could. I called the concierge, begging him to see if there was any way I could get my dress back from the hotel cleaner (there was!). I checked and rechecked the bathroom and the floors, and once I was sure there wasn't anything of mine in the room, I left, already worried about how long it would take to get to this Trastevere place, and how long it would take to get back.

And if anything at all would be set up at our booth while I was gone.

Still sweating, feeling a bit asthmatic, and not even daring to imagine what I looked like, I asked the concierge to call me a cab. As I waited, I tried to calculate whether I had enough money to take a taxi to Trastevere and then back to God knows where north of Rome. I decided I did. One piece of good luck.

The forty-minute ride to Trastevere was beautiful.

We went down busy streets, past monuments and through gardens. At one point we sped past an area that overlooked what seemed to be the whole city of Rome. There was the dome of St. Peter's Basilica, literally shining in the afternoon sun. Revealing my foreigner status completely—though being picked up at a hotel with luggage probably already gave it away—I asked the driver to stop. He obliged, going from about a hundred miles an hour to zero, with a tremendous amount of screeching on the part of the car. I got out and walked up to the edge of the hill; I stood there for a perfectly peaceful moment. The air was warm and breezy, and as I looked out over the vast expanse of the city that was going to be home for the next month and thought how beautiful it was, I told myself that eventually Dick would leave. I'd probably have at least three weeks to enjoy the city without him. I took one last look at the view and hurried back into the cab.

"*Andiamo?*" asked the driver and I said yes, hoping that *andiamo* didn't mean "Should I take you on a three-hour tour of the catacombs?" or "Do you want to go to France?" As we sped down a hill, I noticed a big, white monument on the left. It looked like some sort of stage, with columns at each corner and a big cauldron of fire in the center. Across the top, there was a large inscription, *Roma O Morte.*

"*Dov' e?*" I asked my driver, hoping that if in Italian "*Ciao*" could mean both "hello" and "goodbye" that maybe "*Dov' e?*" could mean "Where is?" and also "What is?"

The driver turned almost completely around in his seat, without slowing down at all, and told me quite enthusiastically, "Ah, si! Is the Fascist Monument! Roma or Death!" He grinned, and raised a clenched fist passionately toward the roof of the car.

Rome or Death. One or the other? I chose Rome. I chose Rome over death. I wouldn't die here because of Dick.

The driver charged me ninety dollars for the trip.

I walked across a narrow street and stood, with my two bags beside me, in front of an iron gate, behind which rose a flight of about forty mossy, very slippery-looking steps. I punched the number I had written down, 3465, onto a keypad by the gate, and it buzzed and opened. I took a deep breath, picked up my bags, went through the gate, and started up the steps.

I didn't have any keys.

How in hell was I supposed to get in if I didn't have any keys? Before completely flipping, which I was quite ready to do, I'd read Amanda's e-mail again. Being at the very end of my very tethered, very frayed rope, I may have missed something about where to pick up keys—from a neighbor's apartment perhaps? That would be okay. In addition to *Dov' e,* I knew how to say *Buon giorno.* Bone jore-no. Good day! I could just knock on the neighbor's door and say, "*Buon giorno!* I'm Jane Laine. Do you have a key for me?" Maybe he'd speak English. Maybe he'd be about thirty-four, tall, dark, dashing, and brilliant. Maybe we would travel through Italy together, all over the country, living off the giant trust fund he had for being a member of royalty.

Right.

I sat down on the damp steps; the fact that my pants were getting wet was secondary to everything else. I turned on my computer, which thankfully had some battery power and went to my downloaded e-mails to look for what I must have missed before. But there was nothing, no mention at all of a Roman soulmate key-bearing neighbor. I walked back through the gates and dragged my bags into the piazza across the street, sure that at least there I would find what I was looking for: a big black T sign with the word *Tabacchi* written underneath. I walked into the store; bought a pack of Gauloises Blondes, which I'd enviously seen everyone smoking in London; and asked also for a *biglietta,* a word I'd heard a million times on the bus and now knew meant "ticket." I walked back to the foot of all those steps with my cigarettes and bus ticket, punched in the numbers again, opened up the gate again, sat down on the wet steps again.

I opened up the pack. I lit the cigarette and inhaled, felt light-headed for a second, felt all the dampness seeping through my pants, and knew I was about to cry. *No!* I told myself as firmly as I could, *I am not going to cry.* I hadn't since leaving on this trip, and I was afraid that if I did, some flood gate of misery would open and I'd be back to crying every day, the way I had after I saw the daisies. There had to be something I could do. I took out my cell phone and looked at it for a minute. It was three o'clock in Italy, nine in New York.

Amanda Cell was first on my cell phone's list of saved names.

"Hello. This is Amanda."

"Amanda, it's Jane."

"Hello, Jane," she said, all false brightness and artificial light. "I am so sorry to hear about the disaster with *Untitled #6*. How devastating for that to happen on your watch!"

"Amanda. Listen. I am outside the apartment complex in Rome and I don't have keys. Do you know where I can find them?"

"Yes, of course," she said sweetly. "I'm sure I included that in my e-mail to you."

"No, actually you didn't. That's why I'm calling you."

"No, I'm quite sure that I included it in the e-mail I sent to you."

"No. *A-man-da*. You didn't."

"I'm not at the gallery right now, just on my way. But I'm positive that if I were at the gallery, and looked in my sent messages folder, and read the e-mail that I sent, that I would see I had included specific instructions about the keys."

"You didn't!" I yelled into the phone, not sorry at all to be yelling at Amanda. The only thing I was sorry about was that Amanda wasn't there so that I could strangle her.

"I'm sure if you read the e-mail—"

"Amanda, why do you think I am calling you?! I don't know where the keys are! Obviously you do! I don't know how else to explain this to you! Please just tell me where they are!"

"Okay, *Jane,*" she said, emphasis on the Jane. "They are under the mat outside the door of the apartment exactly as I wrote in the e-m—"

I thought if it ever came up, I could blame it on the transatlantic cellular connection. I hit the end call button with as much ferocity as I could manage, and made my way up the million steps.

After reaching the top, I walked along a walkway; the palm trees lining it made my mind hesitate in its anger for just a second to notice how beautiful it was. I passed a few doors that weren't marked 12 and then came to the one that was, pulled up the mat in front of it, and found a set of keys. I opened the door and didn't have to wonder at all about whether smoking was allowed in the apartment, because as I walked in, it was surely the smokiest place I'd ever been where people were not actually smoking.

It was as if a party of chain smokers had run out the back door when they heard my newfound key turning in the lock.

That wasn't actually a possibility, though, as there wasn't any back door. The room was square with a very large wooden table in the center. On one wall was a stove; another held a mini-refrigerator, and a mini-freezer hid behind paisley tapestries. Off to one side was a door to a very small bathroom. There was a futon that didn't look as if it would be able to be opened unless the table was moved. There was a rustic charm to the room, except for all the smoke . . . but what was that hissing sound? I thought maybe, while hoping maybe not, that a hot water pipe was about to burst, that all the smoke was actually steam. *Steam that smells smoky?* I scanned the walls for the culprit pipe. What I found instead was a fat, gray tabby cat, crouching with its neck squashed down and its ears pinned back. Its little fangs were visible in its open mouth as it hissed at me. It sat near its litter box, a small pile of cat crap sitting neatly in front of it.

Having lived in a house filled with Schnauzers, I've never spent very much time around cats. I realized I hadn't been missing much. With cautious glances in the direction of the feline, I walked over to the table and picked up a laminated piece of paper.

Dear Tenant,
Bienvenudo a Roma! *I hope that you enjoy your stay here. By now I am sure that you have met Lucia. She is very low maintenance and just needs her water dish changed once a day and her food dish filled twice a day. In the garbage can under the sink, you'll find everything you'll need for litter changing. Please*

change the litter every other day. Please note that Lu-cia's name is pronounced Lu-chi-ah. Please do not call her Loo-see-ah, as that upsets her. She also likes it a lot if you say hello to her.

If you have any problems, the landlady, Mrs. Cugiello, lives in apartment #1 and should be able to help you.

Presto, Francesca

I sat down at the table and smoothed my hair, trying to compose myself, to gather my thoughts. I lit a cigarette because, really, what else could I do? I tried desperately to find my spiritual center. I turned back toward the crazed kitty, tried to smile, and said to her:

"Hello, Lucia."

Because, really, what else could I say?

20

A MOMENT ISN'T VERY LONG

"The tireder you are, the less impressed
you are. With anything."
—Andy Warhol

I didn't get back to the art fair until after six that night.

When I arrived, the *Centro Nazionale per le Arti Contemporanee* was quiet, all the booths seemed to be unpacked, and only a very few people were there, getting ready to leave. I hoped Dick wouldn't be one of the few. I headed toward our booth, knowing I would see crates, bubble wrap, boxes, disorder, and at least three to four hours of setup work ahead of me. *Please no Dick, please no Dick,* I repeated to myself softly, a rhythmic, almost religious chant.

When I got there, I was astonished.

There weren't any crates, or bubble wrap. There were no

boxes, no disorder, and very, very best of all, no Dick. I looked around in awe at the perfectly organized booth, the beautifully placed sculptures, the chrome furniture all in the right places. All the catalogs and press releases were piled in neat stacks on the table. I stood in front of one of the sculptures and as I stared at it, against the backdrop of everything that was so very neat (clap-clap) and clean (clap-clap), I felt the stress of the day melt away. For a moment, I felt happy.

There is a reason why moments are called moments.

As I looked toward the closet, I saw the handle start to turn. Dick was in there. Dick had been forced to set everything up, looking at graph paper diagrams for hours, while working out how to make me wish I'd never been born. Or at least had never taken that first art history class. I looked down at the floor as all my good feelings about the booth being perfect evaporated.

"Well hello there, Jane!"

My frazzled, disjointed mind heard an English accent. *It wasn't Dick. It was Ian!*

"Oh, Ian," I said, so relieved. "Did you do this all by yourself? I'm so sorry—"

"Not at all, Jane. Not at all. And don't worry, Dick left right after you did and I told him I'd be following shortly. No need to worry," he assured me. The way he looked at me then made it seem like he knew exactly what my day had been like. As mad as it made me to picture Dick making sure nothing would be done in my absence, all that anger washed away in the wave of gratitude for Ian that swept over me.

"Thank you so much, Ian. I really owe you," I gushed.

"No, you don't. You don't owe me a thing," he said, and

then laughing added, "But if you insist, why don't we start with dinner?"

I wondered where he got his energy. Didn't he ever feel as completely, fatally tired as I felt right then, standing there all sweaty, frizzy-haired, and wearing wet pants because I'd forgotten to change in my haste to get away from the cat who had only hissed with deeper passion after I said hello to her? "I can't," I told him. "I'm so beat. I think I need to just call it a day."

"Another time, then," he said and smiled.

"Another time."

"At least let me drop you off?"

"Sure, thanks."

As we walked outside together, Ian told me enthusiastically how he had rented a Vespa for the week, and how it had been delivered during the day. He called it a *motorino* and it was like a scooter, maybe a little bigger. He lifted the seat up and took out two helmets. He gave one to me and I put it on and climbed onto the seat behind him. It felt a little strange to have my arms wrapped around Ian, to be so close to him. But as he sped up the Via Flaminia, in the direction of the city, it didn't seem so strange anymore. It seemed okay. We were going very fast, and had I not been so tired, I might have been scared. Had I not been so tired, I might have noticed how warm the air felt even though it was November. I might have noticed all the sights zooming by and realized that I was in Rome, zipping around on a *motorino* with Ian Rhys-Fitzsimmons, the most important artist of the twenty-first century. I might have felt like I was just about the luckiest person in the world.

. . .

I waited until Ian sped off, then walked across the narrow street to the piazza to get a slice of pizza. I brought it up to the apartment and fell asleep almost as soon as I'd finished eating it, not even bothering to move the table to pull out the futon. I slept so soundly that first night that I never stirred while Lucia endlessly sloshed the water out of her dish and continually scratched all the litter out of her box. That night at least, even her loud meows did not disturb me. I only woke when I felt a little paw on my face. Lucia was sitting sweetly on my chest, reaching out to stroke my cheek.

"Hi, Lucia," I said tenderly, her little kitty nose just inches from my own.

Her ears pinned flat, her neck shrank into her body, and she hissed.

I didn't sleep very much after that, but tried to lie as quietly as I could so as not to further anger Lucia. She sat patiently staring at me, and didn't start her cacophony of rousing screeches until after my alarm went off. I cleaned up the litter mess, fed her, refilled her water, wondered what could have happened to her in her kitty past to bring her to this mental state, and left for the art fair, via a bus and a tram.

Dick was there ahead of me, sitting in a chair, sipping coffee.

He told me I was not needed at the press preview, but rather should go back to the city to oversee the installation of Ian's outdoor sculpture, *Untitled: Red.* It would have been nice had he told me a bit earlier, before I had left the city perhaps. But as I headed back out of the building, I thought no matter what, it was most definitely best that he and I stay in different parts of Rome. I saw the shuttle bus pulling up right as I got outside. I saw the two PR bimbos getting off, chirping and chattering to each other, the words *Ian* and *dinner* falling on my ears. I wondered briefly what he could see in them, wondered which of the two he actually dated; couldn't believe he'd date either of them. I settled into a seat on the bus and sat back, preparing to enjoy the sights I'd missed on my previous journeys.

Untitled: Red, a beautiful, grand sculpture, was being installed right at the top of the Spanish Steps, the age-old meeting place of every foreigner in Rome. It would remain for the month that the Art Fair Project was in Italy. Grant Smith, a New York art dealer who also had a gallery in Rome—the gallery our post–art fair exhibit would be held at—was instrumental in arranging all the details and permits with the Italian government.

As I made my way to the Spanish Steps, I introduced myself to the workmen installing the sculpture as best I could: *"Buon giorno!"* I watched as Ian's sculpture rose up into the bright blue sky. It looked beautiful there, between the ancient obelisk and the right side of the steps that curved around and came together and spilled onto the piazza below. I watched people greet each other, snap photos, walk up the steps, walk down them, sit on them. During the lunch break, I walked down the Via Margutta, where Gregory Peck lived in *Roman Holiday,* and felt for a moment just like Audrey Hepburn.

It was almost five by the time the last installer left, by the time the dashing Grant Smith had dashed by, said *"Ciao,"* and darted off. After stopping at the apartment—which wasn't nearly as far away as my taxi driver had made it seem—I headed back to the fair for the opening party. On my way over, I wondered if Dick would tell me to leave, to stand at the top of the Spanish Steps and guard *Untitled: Red* for the rest of the month.

21

I'M SO TIRED

"That one's problem is HE JUST
WANTS TO BE MISERABLE!"
—Andy Warhol

I walked into our booth just as the opening-night party was about to begin. Dick didn't say anything to me, the booth was in perfect order, and everything was in place. Other dealers and the occasional leftover member of the press walked over to compliment Ian and Dick, and everything seemed just fine. Until I heard a sharp intake of breath. Dick was staring in horror at the chrome desk that held press releases, catalogues, and business cards, and where, had they been there, Reese's peanut butter cups would be proudly displayed. He whipped his head toward me, his body still facing the peanut butter cup void. As I stood there, watching his jaw muscles flex under his jowls, I tried to think of something, anything, to say. I willed myself to look away, to do something other than stare at him, egging on his wrath. But I couldn't look away.

"WHERE!" he shrieked. "Where! Where!"

I knew he was shrieking "Where!" exclamation point, and not "Where?" question mark, so I didn't answer him. I watched him claw desperately at his shirt collar, trying to loosen his tie. "I'M SO TIRED!" he wailed, thrashing his head from side to side, his face getting redder and redder. "I'm just so tired! Why doesn't anyone ever listen to me? Why doesn't anyone ever do what I ask? Whydoesntany-oneeverdowhatIask? Whywhy? Why! Victor, Victor, get me a banana juice! Victor, Victor!"

Victor is in Rome? Victor! Oh, how wonderful! How amazing!

But why, I wondered, *hadn't he told me he was coming?*

As Dick finally removed his tie, gasping one final, raspy, "Victor," I realized Victor wasn't anywhere near Rome, about to waltz into the booth, proffering banana juice and goodwill. Dick, in all his hysteria, had just gone with the usual script he referred to in his breakdowns, and that always culminated in a soothing banana juice brought by Victor. For lack of anything better to do, I walked to the bar that was set up at the other end of the building to see what kind of fruit juice they might have. I returned with orange juice that he didn't thank me for.

The duration of the party felt like I'd traveled back in time and it was September again and I was back in New York. If I could really time-travel there would be so many places that I'd *want* to go. I'd want to be there when Leo

Castelli first met Jasper Johns. I'd love to go to one of Andy Warhol's parties. But the one time, maybe the only time, I'd *never* want to visit again is that black September. There wasn't any pointless candy waiting in the closet this time, so I chose the second-best escape I had: standing at the front of the booth, off to the side, where I wouldn't have to talk to anyone.

"And Jane," I heard Ian say, after what seemed hours of self-imposed solitude. At this, I turned, hoping he'd say, "and Jane and I can't wait until you, Dick, go away, you vile, hateful, little man."

"Jane," he said instead, "Dick and I are having dinner at Nico's. It's one of the best restaurants in Rome. Please join us."

As much as I didn't want to eat with Dick, as much as I didn't want to sit through dinner with him treating me like I was invisible, I knew I should go. "Yes, thank you," I said crisply, not daring to look at Dick.

We traveled in a chauffeured car, back to the Spanish Steps, admired the outdoor sculpture, and then settled into our table at Nico's. Ian told Dick how much he liked the restaurant. Dick patted Ian's arm. "You are Ian Rhys-Fitzsimmons. You deserve only the best," he said in a cloying, syrup-coated voice, "and exactly what you want. And those two things are usually one and the same." Dick sat back contentedly as if what he'd just said was the cleverest thing ever.

The food was excellent. I had the most delicious artichoke to start, and then an absolutely perfect pasta. The wine was wonderful; everything in Rome tasted better than it did anywhere else. I was so happy with everything I was eating that it didn't even bother me that during the course of the meal Dick spoke only to Ian. I couldn't believe it when, over coffee, Dick turned to face me and said "Jane." He looked at me as if I were a real person, sitting in a restaurant with him. "I want to talk about vacation schedules," he said.

"Okay," I answered.

He exhaled, "Jane, is it or is it not part of your job to keep track of everyone's vacation time?"

"Yes, it is," I replied and then added, "Dick."

He looked at Ian with a plea for sympathy. Ian stared at him blankly. Dick turned back to me and spoke loudly. "WELL, can I SEE IT?"

"Can you see what?"

"I AM SO TIRED!" he screeched in despair. "Don't you keep a chart or a list?" he demanded. "It makes no sense, no sense at all to keep something like that in your head. You have to write it down! Keep a chart! When I started in this business, I always kept charts and lists and never carelessly neglected to do that!"

"Dick," I said, "I do keep a chart."

"Letmeseeit!"

"It's saved on my computer."

"Letmeseeit!"

"Unfortunately I can't do that at this moment. The comp—"

"Where is the computer? Is the computer not here? Where is the computer?" He moved his head quickly from left to right in an apparent attempt to unearth the location of my computer. "The gallery bought you a laptop, Jane, and I would hope you could appreciate that and bring the laptop with you as you are supposed to. I would hope that you would understand that. Where is the computer? Where?"

"The computer is locked in the closet in the booth, but I—"

"Well, I need to know right now when each staff member took vacation this year, so go and get it. Print the document and leave it for me at the desk of the hotel."

I wanted to remind Dick that the fair was forty minutes away. I wanted to ask him why we had to talk about this tonight, right this minute. I also wanted to tell him that if there was any justice in the world, one day all the bad things he did and said would come back to haunt him. *Because karma, Dick, is a bitch, and instant karma is even worse.* "Right now there are only five of us on staff. I can tell you *exactly* when everyone took their vacation," I said instead.

"I want to see the document," he said dismissively. He turned his attention back to Ian, his face morphing from sneer to smile. "So, Ian. What are your plans for Tuscany?"

"Dick, I must say it seems quite pointless for Jane to travel outside the city on her own. At night. Perhaps this could be taken care of tomorrow?"

Dick's eyes clouded for a minute, then his reptilian mind remembered that it was wise never to disagree with Ian. He turned back to me with pursed lips, "Jane, tell me," exhale, "what you can about the staff vacations."

I was so mad I wanted to spit. What I also wanted to do was leave. But it had been very nice of Ian to step in and stand up for me, and I didn't want him to think I didn't appreciate it. I took a breath and turned toward Dick. "Clarissa took a week last February. Sam took his week in March, and Victor took a week in April. Amanda took a week in July. I'm taking the week between Christmas and New Year's."

My parents were spending Christmas in Colorado; Fideleis has family in Telluride. I hated skiing, but with Telluride being right between Chicago, where we'd be in December, and Santa Fe, where we'd be in January, it worked out perfectly. I would have liked it if the Schnauzers didn't need to visit family for the holidays, so Christmas could have been in New York, but still, I was really looking forward to the break.

"Jane," Dick began, and it actually looked as if he were smiling at me. It was probably just some sort of facial tic. "We're changing our vacation policy. Vacation weeks are going to be taken only in July and August, during the quieter months. Like Amanda did last year. I am sure you will be able to arrange your schedule accordingly."

What? I'd taken the week between Christmas and New Year's off ever since I'd started working for Dick. I thought how next year I wouldn't, and how that would be kind of a drag . . . Then it hit me. "You don't mean this year, do you?" I asked, even though I already knew the answer.

"Yes."

"But that's ridiculous!" I blurted. "I haven't taken a vacation in a year! And I have plane tickets and plans. Everyone else had vacation before you made this policy and—"

And then I just stopped talking. I thought about spending Christmas alone. I felt as if my head were going to spin off. I felt like standing up and screeching for the whole world to hear that I was *just so tired*. Then I got up and left. I walked as quickly as I could out of the restaurant and as soon as I was outside, I felt my eyes starting to sting. I had no idea what to do next, or where to go, or how to get there. I saw Ian's sculpture standing grandly at the top of the Spanish Steps. Without another thought I ran to it. I stood right by it, and looked at it, and slowly I didn't feel quite as frantic. I stared at Ian's sculpture and I felt calmer.

"Jane?"

I turned to see Ian, standing a little way behind me, holding my jacket. I felt stupid then for rushing out of the restaurant.

"Are you all right?" he asked, still standing away from me.

"He just makes me feel so, so, so—"

"So, what?" He walked toward me and handed me my jacket.

"He makes me so mad," I said finally. But it was so much more than that. It was that he made me feel completely pointless. "He makes me feel pointless."

"Well you shouldn't feel that way at all," he said.

"I do, though."

"Keep in mind, then, that everyone feels that way sometimes. Even if they don't work for Dick Reese. Everyone has days when they don't feel so sure of themselves. I know I do," he said softly and then paused for a minute, looking at me.

"Jane, it's all about believing in yourself. Everything is. You have to believe in yourself and put one foot in front of the other and trust that if you do that, if you keep trying, wonderful things are going to come out of it. That's what I do. I just go about whatever it is I am going about and I believe in myself until there aren't any people left who don't believe in me. That's all you need to do."

"It's different for you, Ian." *How could he ever understand?* "You're the person everybody wants on their team. If the world were a dodgeball game, all the teams would be hoping they could pick first, so they could get you. I'm the geeky kid who gets left on the bench, until finally it's just me and someone with glasses from the math club who eats glue."

"Jane. That couldn't be further from the truth. I don't think anyone sees you like that. I certainly don't. And I picked you. Doesn't that count for something?"

"What did you pick me for?" I asked.

"I picked you to work with me on the Art Fair Project. Remember? This little tour we are on?" There was a bit of sarcasm in his voice, but definitely not the Dick Reese belittling and diminishing kind. "I asked Dick for you to accompany me. I didn't ask for Amanda or Victor or Sam or Clarissa. I didn't ask for them because I wanted you. I wanted you to be with me on this project because I think you are bright and I think you handle everything that Dick throws at you as gracefully as possible and I think you are smart and capable. Jane, you've kept everything running smoothly and you have never, not once, made me regret choosing you. Given the chance a million times again, I'd choose you every time."

Oh, God, I thought. "Dick never told me that," I said. "I thought he sent me because I served no purpose at the gallery. Not that I don't think this is a wonderful, unbelievable opportunity," I added, "because I do. I *really,* really do." I wanted him to know how much being on the Art Fair Project meant to me. "Ian . . . what you said just now, that's the nicest thing someone has said to me in a long time."

"Well, I meant every word of it. But I simply can't believe Dick didn't tell you."

"It never made much sense to me, until now, why I was picked."

I couldn't think of anything else to say; Ian saw me as bright and graceful, as smart and capable.

"I'm Ian Rhys-Fitzsimmons. Dick's only going to give me the very best or exactly what I want, and those two things are usually the same," he said and winked.

I looked at the cobblestone street, then up at the sculpture. Wanting to hug Ian yet again, I realized we had been standing in silence for a while. "Thanks," I said.

"Anytime," he said and looked down at his watch. "I don't know about you, but I could really go for a drink."

"I'd *really,* really like that," I smiled, and rolled my eyes for emphasis.

We walked past his sculpture, down the steps toward the Piazza de Spagna.

"And just so you know," he said after a minute, "in school, they never picked me for any teams. I didn't eat glue, but I always carried around graph paper and was frightfully bad at catching any sort of moving object. Jane, no one ever picked me."

"Really?" It had never occurred to me that Ian hadn't always been the center of attention, the best at everything he did.

"*Really,* really," he said and even though I couldn't see his face, I knew he was smiling.

22

YOU SAY GOODBYE
AND I SAY *HELLO*!

"I never read; I only look at pictures."
—Andy Warhol

Dick remained in Rome for the entire first week of the fair.

When he was near me, I was unsure about everything I said, about anything I thought. The fair itself was also disjointed; afternoons were broken up by the designated three-hour siesta when everything closed down—Rome was a city with an official naptime.

The week finally came to an end and Dick was leaving. I wished Ian wasn't leaving, too. The good thing was that Ian would be back, and Dick wouldn't. Ian left first with a "Thanks, and see you in a week" to me, and a "Thanks, and see you in January" to Dick. Dick and I said brief and formal good-byes; then, as he was about to leave the booth, he stopped and turned back. He pulled something from his briefcase

"*This* is *yours,*" he hissed with revulsion.

I wondered what could possibly elicit such extreme disgust, even from a man who spends a large portion of his time expressing varying levels of it. I looked at the object he held away from his body, as if it were contaminated.

It was my copy of *Hello!* magazine. In my crazed rush to get everything out of my room—Dick's room—at the Hassler, I must have left it behind. As I was about to lie, "No, it isn't!" I thought about Ian's sculpture on top of the Spanish Steps, and what he said to me as we stood in front of it. Ian said all I have to do is believe in myself. I stared at Dick's hand for one long minute, then looked right into his eyes. I watched them narrow, and I narrowed my own. As we stood there firmly, facing each other with shrinking eyes, it occurred to me—and honestly, not for the first time—*I might turn into Dick*. "Yes, it is," I said.

It was he who looked away, then turned around and walked off.

Had that been a battle, and had I won it?

The art fair continued in a sporadic and disorganized way, yet somehow things that needed to get accomplished did. In fact, that is exactly how I'd describe all of Rome. There is a beautiful feeling of disorder when you're in the Eternal City.

Each day I would stay at the fair while it was closed for siesta; it didn't make much sense to travel back to my apartment and the troubled Lucia only to return almost as soon as

I got there. Many people stayed during siesta, and I began to walk around the fair, visiting other booths. The day I claimed my *Hello!* magazine, I walked to one I'd never before had the nerve to go into.

Susan Menton has a small but very respected gallery. She represents lesser-known artists than Dick Reese or Karina Kratsch, but she still shows quality, innovative art and always does it with a subtle, understated style. I've always admired her for her taste, but also for another reason. She is the one person who got out. Long before I heard the name Dick Reese, when I was still in college thinking art was all about beauty, not knowing the ugliness that could lurk behind it, Susan had worked for him. Yet unlike the many, many people who had left the Dick Reese Gallery never to be heard from again, Susan got out.

With her reputation and dignity intact.

And she thrived.

As a Dick Reese employee, I'd never been to Menton Fine Art, and had never *dared* to wander into Susan's booth at art fairs. But that was about to change. Arriving, I walked halfway down the length of the Menton Fine Art booth, looking straight ahead. I stopped, took a deep breath, then turned and walked in. Cautiously, I looked at the paintings, while stealing quick glances over to where this person, so famous and revered in my mind, was sitting finishing a phone call. When she hung up she said "Hello."

"Hello," I repeated. "I'm Jane Laine. I work for Dick Reese." I said it quickly, not wanting her to think I was some sort of minion's minion, sent over to spy.

"Oh, do you?" she asked sympathetically.

With those three syllables and the way she raised her eyebrows and smiled as she said them, I felt such a sense of comfort and commiseration that it was all I could do not to run the four or five steps that separated us and throw my arms around her.

"I do," was what I said instead.

"Jane, I was about to go get a cup of coffee. Would you like to join me?"

I'd never before wanted so very much to have a little cup of Italian coffee. We went down the aisle together and turned at the transverse, ordered some coffee, and sat at one of several small tables. We talked and talked, but never about Dick; Susan didn't bring up his name and neither did I. Instead we discussed the exhibition she had brought to Italy, and spoke about what a unique fair it was. She listened to what I said and treated me like an equal. The conversation eventually went in the direction of the Art Fair Project. She spoke glowingly of how she admired Ian's work and his concepts. I agreed with her and really meant it. Though I still didn't fully understand his work, I did feel like I was getting closer to it. I'd come to hold Ian in high esteem, and felt certain that I always should have.

Our coffee break ended and the fair opened back up. As people began to appear in the aisles, we got up to make our way back to our separate booths. We said good-bye and as I walked away, I had the feeling that I'd see Susan Menton again.

23

A LOVE FOR LIFE

*"A place can really make your heart skip a beat,
especially if you have to take a plane to get there."*
—Andy Warhol

Two sculptures sold during the second week of the fair. Occasionally, I would go over and visit Susan, but not too frequently, as I didn't want to be too blatant about fraternizing with the enemy, no matter how nice the enemy was. Though I didn't have anyone to talk to very often, that week was perhaps one of the best I'd spent, because it was when I fell in love with Rome.

The warm weather allowed walking for hours, and I walked all the time. I walked everywhere. Through the narrow streets of Trastevere, to the bustle of Campo dei Fiori just across the river, to the dramatic sweep of the Spanish

Steps to check in on *Untitled: Red*, then over to the vast expanse of the Villa Borghese just beyond the Piazza del Popolo.

Every night after leaving the fair, I'd take the bus back to the city and get off somewhere else, and something incredible would be there. I'd stop for dinner at a place I'd read about or just walk into a trattoria that looked nice. I never thought about gaining weight. Every meal was so delicious. It seemed truly pointless to think about something as trivial as being skinny or fat. I loved spending time in Rome, and I learned that I loved spending time with myself.

I didn't mind eating dinner alone. In New York, I always felt sorry for people I saw alone at restaurants. In London, I was scared to try it. But in Rome, I loved it. I would sit and watch all the people in the restaurant, or walking by in the street, and try to put together words and phrases I remembered from my Berlitz tape with all the sounds I heard around me.

I didn't move back to the Hassler after Dick vacated it. Aside from Lucia, I liked Trastevere too much. I learned it was considered the cool area, the hip area, the "even though there are heroin addicts on the streets it's the place to be" area. It felt more real to be a part of a neighborhood than to stay in a hotel. I liked the bohemian, tourist-free environment. I loved the narrow streets that seemed miles away from the traffic and crowds of the central city. I liked the bar, Ombre Rosso, that I passed on the way home to my apartment, the same group always gathered around the same table, drinking wine and smoking and laughing. Grant Smith's gallery was also in Trastevere, so it was in fact more convenient for me during the second half of our stay.

Grant Smith's gallery was in the courtyard of a quiet area of mostly apartments and restaurants. It was not where you would picture a cutting-edge, contemporary gallery to be. Yet Smith's New York reputation as an innovator had followed him to Rome. Everyone was interested in what he had to show, and his large gallery space, with an orange tree–filled courtyard behind it, was always busy.

As I went about setting up our exhibition the day before it opened to the public, out of the corner of my eye, I saw a blur of purple and yellow zoom by. Ian was back, right on time to help with setting up. He came over to me first, said hello and asked how the second week in Rome had been. I told him it had been wonderful and as I started to fill him in on activity at the fair, I realized he had asked how *Rome* had been, not just how the *fair* had been. Not everything was work with Ian. What was it he'd told me? Everything somehow funneled into work. It was refreshing that Ian cared about more than whether his sculptures sold.

"Ian! Good to see you back," said Grant Smith, emerging from a back room. He wore black-frame glasses just like Ian's and had a similar fashion sense, though not as daring. The two men shook hands and by the way they spoke to each other, it was evident that they'd known and liked each other for years. "Nope. Nope. We close up every day from two to five." Grant answered a question Ian had asked.

"And open until?"

"Six," Grant replied with a smile and a wink at the two really enthusiastic people who worked at his gallery, then said he'd see us tomorrow, and left.

I liked him. I wanted to work for him. Maybe I could

move to Rome forever, get rid of the cat, and stay on in my very small and smoky, but still rustic and charming Trastevere apartment. I could walk to the gallery every day through the market stalls that filled the piazza adjacent to my street, and I'd make friends with that group of people always smoking and drinking at the Ombre Rosso.

With Ian returned and the city at hand, I had company for dinner and now added big, carefree lunches to my list of wonderful things about Rome. One night, after a dinner that included chicory and fennel salad and fettuccine with truffle oil, as we sat together sipping our Limoncello against a backdrop of lemon-yellow walls, Ian asked me, for the first time, about Jack.

"Do you still see that tall Texan fellow who used to come round to all the openings? Jack, is it?" he asked casually.

Jack's name turned something around in my stomach. I paused for a moment to let the sick feeling pass. It passed much more quickly than it ever had before. I looked at Ian and part of me wanted to tell him everything that had happened. I wanted to tell him that I hated daisies. "Yes. It's Jack. Was Jack," I corrected. "No, we don't see each other anymore."

"Oh?" he said, and there was a question mark there.

"It just didn't work out," I said, instead of "He broke my heart into a million pieces." Ian didn't need to know that since those daisies, I've wondered if not everyone is meant to be in love.

"It's hard," he said and the way he said it, the way he

looked at me, I thought for a split second that I had just said everything out loud.

"What about you? Is it working out or not working out with anyone?" I asked lightly, steering the topic away from myself, wondering if he'd tell me all about the PR bimbi, and whether he was dating the thin blonde or the other one. Maybe he'd even tell me about the beautiful and breathy Karina Kratsch. But before he spoke, I figured he was probably far too discreet.

"I don't know, Jane," he said, nudging at a fork with his thumb. "Maybe I'm too project-oriented . . . too analytical. I tend to concentrate on things, dissect them, pick them apart so they stop being what they originally were to me. I like to think that if I am ever with the person I'm supposed to be with, all the things that break everything apart won't happen any longer. All I know is that I've never quite made it for a year in a relationship. The rest of it, I don't bloody know."

Even Ian, with all of his success and with the entire world praising him, had been hurt and disappointed and disillusioned. What happened to me wasn't so unique. I couldn't picture him placing a relationship on graph paper and analyzing it to death. But if he did do that, if that was the way he was, was that so terrible? "Finding happiness with someone is a really hard thing. But you will," I told him, just like everyone told me. "You'll find that person and be happy for much longer than a year."

"Yes, well, I like to think so. It's funny, actually. I've seen your copy of *Wuthering Heights* and there's a line in there that I've always remembered that reminds me of all of this."

"Really?" I asked.

A flicker of amusement crossed his eyes, but he left it alone. "Yes. Let me think for a moment," he said and paused. "Okay, I don't know if I've got it quite right. It's nearer to the beginning. Mr. Lockwood is talking to Nelly about the moors and I think he says, "I could fancy a love for life here almost possible; and I was a fixed unbeliever in any love of a year's standing.""

I wanted to look at him then as if I understood exactly what he meant. I wanted to nod enthusiastically and say, "Yes, yes, exactly." But instead I said, "I'm sorry?"

"You're not following?" he asked.

"I'm not sure."

"It's nothing, really," he said, his face getting a little red, "It's just always stayed with me. That line. That discovery of something, someone, that can change everything, take away all the doubts you had resigned yourself to believe . . ."

He trailed off into silence, and I wanted it for him so badly—I wanted him to find everything he ever wanted. "Ian, you'll find it. I'm sure, as sure as I've ever been," I said quietly.

"Well, maybe," he added with a wink, "maybe you are right and I will find someone with whom happiness outlives a year. Maybe I will find my moors."

Before I went to sleep that night, under the accusing, watchful eye of Lucia, I looked through *Wuthering Heights*, scanning the earlier conversations between Mr. Lockwood and Nelly until I found what I was looking for.

I could fancy a love for life here almost possible.

I wasn't surprised at all to see that he had remembered the quote verbatim.

Ian's departure the next day alerted me to the fact that there was only one more week left in Rome. Time went by quickly, and before I knew it I was saying a sad goodbye to Lucia, putting my key in the door for the last time, and walking back down those forty slippery steps.

Soon I was sitting on another plane, next to Ian, who was proudly showing me his ticket as if he were a child who had just won a prize. "Look. Eight hours," he said, all teeth and wide eyes. "See." He handed me his ticket as if the news were a phenomenon.

"Yes. It's an eight-hour flight," I acknowledged, nodding and speaking slowly, as if to a person on his way to an asylum.

"And *then*," he said excitedly, suspense built into the *then*, "two hours' layover in New York *and* three hours to Chicago."

"Yes," I said again as he gloated next to me.

"Yes," he nodded, smiling happily, eyes wide.

I couldn't imagine why Ian was acting like a freak, then reminded myself that I had promised never to judge him and his zealousness unfairly again. I was simply in a bad mood because we were leaving Rome. It wasn't at all like leaving New York. When I left New York, I knew I'd be back and I knew exactly when. But now, I had no idea. I'd thrown all of my change into the Trevi Fountain and I believed I'd be back, I felt certain I would be, but I knew it wouldn't be soon and right then, not soon seemed to be as long as forever.

As the plane took off, I didn't even think about it crashing; I just thought about Rome and how much it would always mean to me. I tried to look forward to Chicago but didn't know how Chicago in December could be looked forward to. I tried to muster up some excitement for my bridesmaid's dress, which would be waiting for me at the hotel. I tried to think how I would be the best bridesmaid ever, a true angel of happiness spreading sunshine and light everywhere I went. I looked out the window at everything getting smaller and I got that feeling where my throat closes up and my eyes start to sting.

"Jane, what is it?" Ian asked.

"Nothing, nothing," I said, quickly wiping my eyes, making sure no tears had escaped, embarrassed that I'd almost been crying and wondering how he'd seen it right away.

"Are you sure?" he asked.

"I'm sure," I said and I thought how in Rome there hadn't been any dating. In this most romantic city, I'd managed to forget all about it. I hadn't felt anxious that everybody had someone but I hadn't found him yet. "It's just . . ." I added.

"Just what?" he asked.

"Rome. It's . . ."

"Yes?"

"It's just that I could fancy a love for life there almost possible."

"Jane," he said quietly, "I know exactly what you mean."

And I didn't doubt for a second that he did.

24

THE ANGRY BABY HEAD DIET

> "Weight isn't important the way the
> magazines make you think it is. I know
> a girl who just looks at her face in the
> medicine cabinet mirror and never looks below
> her shoulders, and she's four or five hundred
> pounds but she doesn't see all that."
> —Andy Warhol

The Navy Pier Art Fair
Chicago, Illinois

The good news was that after a long flight with movies to
watch and lots of interesting conversation, landing in New
York didn't feel all that bad. There was something comforting about seeing the U.S. Customs signs when we got off the

plane, and as Ian and I went again to separate lines for immigration, it felt really good to be back in the United States. It felt like I was home.

The bad news was that as soon as we got outside into the bone-freezing arctic air in Chicago, I didn't feel like I was home; I just felt cold. Then, when we got to the hotel, Elizabeth's bridesmaid dress was waiting for me, as she said it would be. Strangely, it was too small. I couldn't zip it up. I hoped that an e-mail would help, that surely the bridesmaid dress people would be able to see reason.

Mail to: customerservice@sabrinabridesmaids.com

From: planejane6@hotmail.com

Re: Bridesmaid's Dress for Elizabeth Barber's Wedding / Size Issue

To Whom It May Concern at Sabrina Bridesmaids Dresses, Inc.:

I recently received my bridesmaid dress for Elizabeth Barber's wedding and it appears there has been some mistake. The dress doesn't seem to have been made according to the measurements I sent. It is at least a size too small for me. Perhaps more. Obviously, I am quite concerned about this, because I cannot zip up the dress. I see there are several labels here marked "No Refunds, No Exchanges," but I wanted to know if there is any possible way that I could exchange my dress for a larger size, as obviously this is a bizarre occurrence. I will greatly, greatly appreciate any help that you can offer. Please let me know as soon as possible what my options are. I can be

reached by phone at 917/555-4994 or by e-mail at planejane6
@hotmail.com

Yours sincerely,
Jane Laine

Ian and I met in the lobby restaurant for a quick lunch,
then bundled into our hats and scarves and gloves and coats
and made our way out into the cold. It wasn't like Rome;
there was neither adventure nor excitement nor new things to
be discovered at every turn. It was just a straight line from
the hotel to Navy Pier, where the fair was being held. And
damn, was it cold!

The days seemed to meld together in a peaceful routine. I
would start every morning by admonishing the evil spirits I
was sure were in the closet of my hotel room, making my
clothes shrink so that everything was tight. Then Ian and I
would meet for breakfast before heading over to the art fair.
Repeating "La la la la la la la" over and over again in my
head was the absolute only way to not think about the fact
that the air outside was colder than anything, anything ever
at all. "La la la la la la la," was the only way to make it alive
on the Everest-like expedition from the hotel, across the street,
to the fair.

At the fair we would be visited by the fawning PR bimbos, occasional clients—two bought sculptures—and we would
look at paintings of angry baby heads . . . mocking, accusing

baby heads. Our booth was across the aisle from Gallery Lanue, a strange—creepy if you ask me—gallery that handles representational art. Like our gallery, they were only showing works by one artist. Unlike our gallery, the artist being shown was clearly *not* the greatest living artist. Grétar Ingvarsson was possibly quite close to being the polar opposite of the greatest living artist. Ingvarsson's group of paintings showed severed heads of deformed babies, with ghastly piercing eyes that stared right at you. Ian, who never says anything negative about someone's creativity, commented that Ingvarsson is from Iceland and Icelanders are a very depressed people.

If the weather in Iceland is anything like the weather in Chicago, I can see why.

Ian didn't go anywhere after the first week like he had at the other fairs. I wondered why he had chosen to stay at this fair, although I was happy for his company. The blur of days moved ahead, and despite the comparative boredom, I liked the serenity and the peacefulness. Eventually, looking at the angry baby heads became so unappealing that I lost my appetite and miraculously, the evil spirits left my closet and my clothes started to get a bit looser. The bridesmaid dress was close to zipping; that was good, because the dress people would not give me a bigger size. In the American mind-set that I was firmly back in, the impending return to my regular size was reason enough for celebration, but I had another. Turns out that even though the new Dick Reese policy prohibited winter vacationing, I wouldn't be spending the holidays alone after all. Rather than going to Telluride as originally planned, my family was heading to a house that they had rented in Santa Fe, so we were all going to be celebrating Christmas together. Elijah has family in Taos.

I got great news from Victor that first week in Chicago.

"Jane! Oh, honey!" he sang through the phone one night. "I'm so happy and he's just the best and we get along so well and the big yellow circle shines in the sky every single day!"

"Oh, Victor!" I said, so happy to hear him so thrilled, so in love.

"And . . ." he said, full of suspense, "I'm gonna do the Love Calculator!"

"You're going to do what?" I gasped, shocked and instantly worried. The Love Calculator is a Web site; you type in your name and someone else's and then "Dr. Love" tells you what the chances are that a relationship between the two names will work out. It is so important, more important than I can convey, *not* to type in your name with someone else's if you're not ready. The Love Calculator must be treated with reverence and used cautiously, only at the right time. Getting back a low percentage on a new relationship can certainly doom it.

"I just know it's gonna be 90 percent or higher!"

"Victor, you know the rule, you made the rule! Never, never type in your name too early! If it's too soon, that bad number will be out there! Remember Arthur?" I said, reminding him of an unfortunate episode he'd described to me, the very first time he'd shown me the Web site. Arthur, in a frenzy of poor judgment, had crazily typed in his name with the names of four guys he'd had "great first dates" with. Not one had come back higher than 26 percent. He'd called Victor in a panic, but Victor showed no pity: "Not one of those guys is ever going to call ever again," he'd said.

And not one of them ever did.

The Love Calculator is a powerful, powerful tool.

"Don't do it! It's too soon! You're not ready for the Love Calculator!" I warned him, repeating the warnings he had often admonished me with.

"Oh, live a little, baby!" he said and hurried off the phone.

Hanging up, even though I couldn't quite support his plan, I hoped that Victor and his new love would equal 100 percent. That's the number, by the way, that comes back if you type in Kate's maiden name with Diego Martinez. Never one to listen to my own warnings, I turned on my computer and, like a woman possessed, went right to lovecalculator.com. I typed Jane Laine very slowly into the space marked "Name of person 1." I stared for a while at the empty space for the second name. All that inviting whiteness, just waiting to be filled. As if led by Dr. Love himself, I typed one single letter: *I*

Horrified, I quickly closed my browser.

Not enough. I shut down my laptop, unplugged it, and put it away in its bag. As I placed the bag securely underneath my bed, as far as it could go, I reminded myself about Karina Kratsch and the PR bimbi. I reminded myself that Ian, wonderful, amazing Ian, was a cherished friend and that was surely all. As I hurried to the bathroom as much to wash up for bed as to be as far away from my computer as possible, I consoled myself with the knowledge that the Love Calculator can, as sure as anything else in this world, make you crazy.

25

INVESTMENT BANKERS
ARE MY WEAKNESS

"Being single is best but everyone
wants to fall in love."
—Andy Warhol

Why, why, why have an art fair in Chicago in the winter? Why doesn't the city simply fly itself south? Chicago really is too cold. By the last day of the fair, everything was too cold for me. On our last trek from the hotel to the pier, as my eyes teared and icicles started forming on the scarf that was wrapped around my neck, I "La la la la la-ed" and thought of Christmas in Santa Fe and warm weather. I thought of beautiful light and Georgia O'Keeffe–inspiring landscapes, just ten days away.

We hustled into the warmth of the fair, and as the door

closed behind us and we unwrapped our faces, Ian said, "Chicago, I have decided, is boring."

He was wearing a grass-green-and-white checked shirt with a lime-green tie. *An attempt at entertaining himself, perhaps?* I decided against asking him as much. "It isn't as boring as it is cold," I offered instead.

"Yes, that's exactly it, Jane. The cold makes everything infinitely less enjoyable. When I was here before and it was warm, I actually very much enjoyed Chicago. Now it's just too cold to enjoy anything."

We'd been on the road for two and a half months and were both feeling tired, slightly worn out, and a bit restless. We headed to the booth and commiserated a bit about freezing in Chicago for ten more days, but also agreed that the fair had gone as well as the others. We reminded ourselves that the Christmas-shopping art collectors were bound to make the gallery portion of our stay busy. We talked about European versus American appreciation for Ian's sculptures, and how he had begun to think it was all a matter of promotion. It was interesting, the way he was able to see his work so commercially and still have it mean something to him. I thought how it must be very hard for him to be objective about something that was so clearly an extension of himself.

"Today is Tuesday, right?" Ian asked, suddenly.

"It is."

"Okay, then, I've got it. The Art Institute is open until nine on Tuesdays. The fair closes at five and all the pieces are small. We can have them packed up and off by six, six-thirty at the absolute latest. I say we go to the Art Institute tonight as soon as we're done. It's been years since I've seen *A Sunday*

Afternoon on the Island of La Grande Jatte and it's my all-time favorite. What do you say? We could have dinner at the Tea Room after? Only boring people are bored, right?"

Suddenly, instead of standing with Ian, I was holding a parasol and wearing a petticoat on the Island of La Grande Jatte. I was with beautiful, elegant people standing on a green grassy hill, people who resembled shapes. Circles and rectangles and arches and curves that weren't even shapes, but simply dots, tiny points of color. Everything came from those tiny points of color. The Georges Seurat painting Ian just named was the reason I had majored in art history. To look at *A Sunday Afternoon on the Island of La Grande Jatte* makes me feel completely, peacefully happy. It has always been my favorite; I had a print of it in my room when I was growing up. I still remember looking at it, wanting so badly to jump into the picture, to become elegant, to become pastel, to become shapes and dots and flecks of color until I was *really,* really part of something. It wasn't really such a coincidence that we had the same favorite painting; *A Sunday Afternoon* is a favorite of so many people. It's also the unofficial mascot of the Art Institute of Chicago. Still, it was nice to know I had the same favorite something as the world's greatest living artist. "Ian, that sounds like a great plan. You're on."

The day was very quiet. No visits from the PR bimbi, who had been there only for the first week, which was fine by me. A few people strolled around but the excitement was over and probably, like the last day of most fairs, nothing was going to happen. Ian thought he'd walk around the pier to look at the other galleries now that there weren't any crowds. "Ian, you should," I said. So he wouldn't feel obligated to sit around the booth with me, I assured him, "Nothing is going to happen."

He went off and I sat at the desk and twirled my hair and stared at the angry dead baby heads across the way. It seemed that the leader angry baby was mocking me. For lack of anything else to do, I went to the closet and got the bag of mini peanut butter cups to refill the dish at the front of the booth—too many spies could report their absence to Dick. It was after I straightened up and turned around that someone crashed into me. And that's when I met Ryan.

I was pretty sure I had seen him before. In New York. I thought he might have come to the gallery once or twice and maybe I'd seen him walking around at the Fall Art Fair in September. I guessed that he was a collector.

"Sorry about that." He smiled.

Six feet tall, blond hair, blue eyes to go with his blue shirt, khaki pants and a brown belt that perfectly matched his brown suede Ferragamo shoes. He touched my arm and electricity went through it. I couldn't take my eyes off him. I saw the high-tech cell phone clipped to his belt and noticed that *Chase Corporate Challenge: Central Park, New York* was stitched onto his over-the-shoulder tote bag. I realized I was very possibly looking at a very dangerous subspecies of the single New York man: The Investment Banker. Though often handsome, frequently charming and successful, these bankers, I know, are not to be trusted. The part of my heart that knew I had already been hurt way too much by a tall and slick, well-dressed and smooth-talking, handsome and confident, all-

American man, pleaded with me to look away from the light. But the rest of me surrendered to the fact that I was standing no more than two feet away from my weakness. If they aren't tall, or if they wear cutting-edge clothes, I can walk away. But the man facing me was tall and his clothes could easily have been from two years ago. I was helpless in the face of it: tall, preppy, banker boys are my kryptonite. It has nothing to do with the job—it's the uniform and the type of corn-fed man that wears it that makes me weak in the knees.

"Ryan Dennison." He extended the hand that had just brushed against my arm. Just short of licking my lips, I pictured him in a navy blue blazer and all my insecurities and fears and war wounds, along with any lessons I learned along the way, melted like butter. I forgot about all the less than desirable guy's guy qualities that might be lurking underneath the Brooks Brothers veneer: the fraternity brothers, the endless televised sporting events, the fishing trips, and the Sundays upon Sundays spent golfing with the boys. I forgot about all of that as soon as I saw this guy who looked like someone had plucked him off of a farm in Indiana and sent him to Harvard Business School. I thought instead how Kate's Diego is an investment banker *and* a wonderful husband and father. I hoped against hope that maybe Ryan Dennison was part of a rare subset: The Investment Banker with a Soul.

"Jane Laine," I said, shaking his hand and thinking, *Jane Dennison doesn't sound half bad.*

"Nice to meet you, Jane Laine. I really like the smaller-scale sculptures. Has Dick Reese always represented Rhys-Fitzsimmons?"

The only thing better than a tall, preppy guy is a tall preppy guy who knows about art! I focused on his blue eyes and gave him the best supercharming smile and the best hair flip that I felt safe attempting simultaneously. "Yes. Actually, for eight years now." I tilted my head, smiled with fewer teeth, and looked out from underneath my eyelashes, impressing even myself with the seamless execution of my flirtation acrobatics. "Ian—Mr. Rhys-Fitzsimmons's first one-man show and first group exhibition in New York were both at Dick Reese Gallery. Before that, however, he was in several student shows in the MFA program at Yale." I thought I sounded smart and knowledgeable.

"What do you think of his work?"

Rather than go into something about dynamism and the relevance of the chosen materials juxtaposed against the colors, I decided instead to say what I believed; the one thing I had thought all along, and that seemed to prove itself again and again the more time I spent around Ian's work. "I think the sculptures are very beautiful. I think they have a remarkable power to bestow happiness on their viewers."

"Well said," said Ryan.

I could feel myself blush and thought, *"Well said."* I wondered if maybe my biggest problem with Ian's work all along had been not listening to what I felt, to what I believed to be true. And just like that, I got it.

Ian's work is so spectacular because of the way it makes people *feel*.

And everyone likes it so much because the way it makes them feel is *happy*.

I had understood it all along. I hadn't needed art theory

and methodology and art historical context in order to understand it. The answer had been right inside me, all I had to do was trust myself and believe in myself enough to find it. *I get it,* I thought. *I always got it!* Thankfully, Ryan was busy looking at *Untitled #17,* so it didn't seem strange that I hadn't answered him. I hadn't been able to, because I was too distracted by all the screaming from the stadium. A little person inside my head, a different miniature version of myself from the one I had met before, had put on a red-and-white cheerleader uniform. She had grabbed some pom-poms and was out in the middle of a football field screaming, "FINALLY!"

A full-house, packed crowd was screaming back to her. She jumped up and did a split in the air. The crowd was wild. One section of the stadium was standing up, their arms over their heads. They were doing the wave! "FINALLY! FINALLY!" the crowd screamed along, and the whole stadium was dancing and hugging and flailing their arms overhead. I couldn't believe it! Not ten minutes ago, I had told Ian that nothing was going to happen, but instead *everything* had happened! As the cheerleader put down her pom-poms, I was able to turn my attention back to Ryan and ask him if he was from New York.

"I am," he said. As the stadium settled down and the crowd took their seats, I thought that maybe, very quietly and unobtrusively, the cheering might go on forever.

As I had thought, Ryan was a banker and was in Chicago on a business trip. Being between meetings, he had come over to the pier to look around. He said he had been to the Fall

Art Fair in September and on the rare trip he was able to take to the Chelsea galleries, he always made it a point to stop by the Dick Reese Gallery. We talked a little bit about New York, and he told me he lived on the Upper West Side. Maybe it wouldn't be so bad to set foot on the opposite side of the park again. Suddenly it seemed there might be things on the Upper West Side other than bad memories.

"How long have you been in Chicago?" he asked.

"Two weeks. Ten days to go."

"I thought I saw something that said this was the last day of the fair?"

I told him it was, and then explained the Art Fair Project. "We're opening up a show tomorrow night at David Dabney Gallery on North Michigan. Some of these sculptures will be there, and some that haven't been exhibited yet. All of them smaller scale."

He smiled again and I loved his teeth.

"I'm going to take this price list with me, Jane," he said. "If I give you my card, would you call me if anyone has their claws in #17? It's the one I'm really interested in. I should wait until after the first of the year to make any big purchases, though."

He handed me his business card after he wrote his cell phone number on the back. On top of everything else, I might be selling something!

"Jane," he said as I put his card in my pocket. "I know it's not much advance notice, but I'm only here for two days. There isn't any way that you might be free tonight, is there? I'd love to take you to dinner."

"I'd like to go to dinner. Thanks."

"Great," he said. "Where are you staying?"

The rest of the day went by as quickly as it could, considering that no one else came into the booth. At five, the fair officially closed and trucks drove in and temporary walls started coming down, art handlers arrived, and bubble wrap was everywhere. Just as Ian had said, the sculptures were packed up and on their way before six. I had more than an hour before Ryan would call. Then Ian looked up from a box he was writing on to say that he was really looking forward to the Art Institute, and I realized that I was a huge idiot.

"Oh, God. Oh, Ian. I'm so sorry. I completely spaced and I made plans to go to dinner with . . ." I didn't want to say "this guy," because I didn't want Ian to think I was trolloping around the art fair making dates with random passersby. I also didn't want to say, "this guy," because I felt bad about blowing him off for someone I didn't even know. Yet. *Maybe I should call Ryan and cancel?* But there had been sparks and there had been electricity . . . "A client," I said sheepishly. "With a client," I repeated more assertively, and told myself that, technically, it wasn't a lie.

I thought that maybe Ian would be mad at me, that he might think I was a flake, but he looked up and he didn't look angry. For a split second he looked very sad. And for the split second after the second he looked so sad, my eyes started to sting and I felt like I was going to cry. I couldn't comprehend why I was so deeply out of touch with my emotions that I was going to cry clear out of nowhere. But then, in a flash, Ian's eyes were twinkling and he winked at me. He walked over to me and punched me very lightly on my arm, like I was his buddy, and I decided I must have imagined he looked sad.

"Don't feel bad, Jane. We've got another ten days in Chicago. We'll do it another time. Not a big deal."

"Oh, Ian, thanks," I said, relieved. "But really, I am sorry. I don't usually do things like this. It's just . . ." I trailed off because I didn't know what to say.

"Is he quite cute, then?" Ian winked again and he really was being so very cool about the double booking that there wasn't any reason not to tell him the truth.

"*Really,* really cute," I told him, kissed him quickly on the cheek, grabbed my coat and scarf, and hurried back out into the cold and back to the hotel to get ready.

26

THESE ARE A FEW OF
MY FAVORITE THINGS

"There are so many songs about love."
—Andy Warhol

At seven, I was dressed and ready to go.

I had on the runner-ups in the best black pants competition, refusing to think of the best pair, and my black pointy boots. On top I wore a black cashmere sweater. I took one last look in the mirror and thought all the black and the boots made me look taller and thinner. I felt confident. I also had that pre-date nervousness I think I'll never shake no matter how very, very old I get. Even though I had given Ryan my cell phone number, I called down to the desk to make sure there was call waiting in the room. There was, so I dialed Kate's cell.

"Hello, Janie!" she sang, knowing it was me from the 312 area code that flashed up on her phone's screen.

"Hello, Katie!" I sang back. "Now promise me, promise me that we won't talk about dinner in Miami because I don't want to jinx it."

"I promise—what's up?"

"Well, nothing . . . yet. But there were sparks and he's tall and he's cute and I met him at the art fair and he's from New York and we're going out tonight!"

"Yae! What's his name?"

"Ryan. Ryan Dennison," I said proudly.

"Oooo. Does he look like Ryan O'Neal?"

"No, but cute. Really cute. And he likes art, and seems smart, and oh my God, Kate I CAN'T believe I forgot to tell you!" I exclaimed, just to the right of squealing. "I think I understand Ian's artwork. I think it all makes sense!"

"No!"

"Yes!"

"What does it mean?" she squealed right back at me.

"He makes me happy!"

"What?"

"It makes me happy!"

"Oh. I thought you said, 'He makes me happy.'"

"No, no. I said *it* makes me happy. It does. That's what I thought all along and I was right!"

"I'm so happy for you, Janie. And sooo excited about your date tonight. Call me at breakfast and tell me all about it!"

"Thanks! I'm excited, too. But I can't talk about it at

breakfast because I'll be with Ian and I don't want to talk about going on a date in front of him."

"Why not?" she asked.

"Because. I don't," I said a little too quickly, almost snappy. Looking at the clock, I saw that it was exactly seven. "Okay, honey, I am going to go because he should be calling any minute. Once we're settled in at the new gallery, I'll phone and tell you all about it! Bye!"

"Bye, have fun!"

Ryan was standing at the bar with a clear drink when I walked into the dark, very New York–feeling restaurant where he had made reservations. He kissed me on the cheek and asked if I wanted a drink before we sat down. I ordered a glass of red wine, gave away my coat, and climbed onto a bar stool. He smiled over at me and took a sip of his drink. "Oh, wait. What am I doing?" he asked, then held his glass toward me for cheering.

"Cheers," we both said, and I thought it was sweet.

We talked about New York, and where we'd been before we got to New York, all the standard first-date things. Slowly, we gave and took all the little tests. The hostess came and asked if we wanted to sit down and he looked at me first to see if I wanted to. After I nodded, we followed her to the table. And then . . . I felt like I was sitting across from a good thing. He told me how he'd like to retire from investment banking by the time he was forty and teach English somewhere; I told him I hadn't wanted to go on this trip, but how it had been such a great experience that from now on I would always think twice before I automatically discounted something as not worthwhile. We talked about his growing up on a farm, well in a midwestern suburb—he didn't really grow up on a farm—and how far away it seemed from Wall Street. We talked about the Art Fair Project and how in the art world, nothing ever seems very far away from Chelsea. Then, as I noticed that we were the last people left in the restaurant, Ryan leaned toward me. "What are you doing tomorrow?" he asked quietly, smiling.

"We're setting up at the gallery for the exhibition."

"Nothing too strenuous?"

On a strenuous scale of one to ten, an exhibition setup is a ten; especially since we set up all day, then have an opening party at night. "No, nothing too strenuous," I answered.

"Great, then. Would you like to get a drink somewhere nearby? These guys seem to want to get out of here," he said, nodding toward the waiters, who indeed seemed to be willing us to leave.

Outside was absolutely freezing and thankfully we went to a bar just two doors down. I had a super-rare feeling, as though I were on the perfect date. If I could have, I would have asked whoever is in charge of these things to let me stay on Michigan Avenue with this tall, handsome, well-dressed, smart, and charming man forever.

"Top ten favorite things to do?" he asked, once we had found our seats and ordered drinks.

"What?" I said, even though I had heard him.

"What are your top ten favorite things to do?" he repeated.

"Ummmm."

"I'll start," he said, and I was relieved. I worried that this question was really a way to start talking about sex. I hoped it wasn't.

"Sleeping late on Sundays," he offered.

Good, I thought, *this is going to be more of a Von Trapp, raindrops-on-roses-and-whiskers-on-kittens sort of game.* Unless he adds "with some really hot babe with a killer rack" onto the end of his sentence. That would be bad. I didn't say anything for a few seconds, to be certain he wasn't going to add anything sexual to his tame statement. "Mmm. Sleeping late on Sundays is great." I mentally hopped off the bar stool, ran out into the street, grabbed my mind out of the gutter, and dashed quickly back inside. "Going to the beach," I offered.

"Yeah, that's good," he agreed. "Ah, a big cup of Starbucks in the morning."

"I love that!" I said and I started to feel really warm, like I might melt. "Seeing the sunrise."

"Nice," he said softly and moved closer to me.

"Yeah," I said and breathed in and felt how close he was to me and I leaned in a little bit more and closed my eyes. He reached over and put his hand on my knee and I could feel him breathing.

"Playing with puppies."

What? "I'm sorry?" I said.

"Playing with puppies," he said again, this time more enthusiastically, leaning back on his stool. Had he just been about to kiss me and then been distracted by puppies? Or was I just leaning in and closing my eyes completely out of context? There was no way to tell, so I sat up too and returned his enthusiastic, puppy-playing-induced grin.

"They are just soooo cute," he added. "Puppies!"

No straight man would list playing with puppies as his third favorite thing. It couldn't be his third favorite. It couldn't. What about watching football? Or closing a really big deal? Or going on a fishing trip? Playing with puppies? Come on; only a gay man would say playing with puppies! I wished he had just looked at me and said, "Banging a really hot babe with a killer rack."

Ryan was looking off into the distance, no doubt recalling running through a meadow in knee pants and suspenders with a pack of puppies and a butterfly net. I tried to make sense of everything. Harvard Business School and Wall Street must be extremely unaccepting worlds. It must not be easy to be gay in those worlds. I couldn't even begin to imagine how different a job in the financial world must be from a job in the art world. I felt bad for Ryan; I understood and empathized with his plight. However, I didn't want to be his beard. "Damn it all to hell," was the only thing left in my head by the time he came back to the present to tell me, "It's your turn."

Every single molecule of the evening was irreversibly altered from the word *puppies*. I finished the last sip of my drink and ordered another. I folded my hands in front of me and said, "Smoking one cigarette with a drink but being able to forget about it after and not go back to smoking the next day." *Why lie?*

"I love that," he said as his eyes lit up.

"Really?"

"I do. I mean, I'm not a smoker. I was, once, but not anymore and I don't, you know, have packs with me and don't ever want to go back to it, but sometimes just that one cigarette with a drink is so good. As long as it's just one. What I do is, I smoke Merit Ultra Lights, not as much nicotine in them so much less risk of getting hooked," he said quickly, as if unburdening a secret he'd been carrying forever.

"Me, too," I said as something inside me relaxed. "Me, too, exactly."

And we looked at each other and our eyes met and we were like two long-lost lovers first spotting each other across a crowded room. Well, not quite, but there is this connection between two delusional smokers, living their smoking lives in denial, that is very strong. He put his hand on my shoulder and there was all the electricity that had been there before. He rubbed his hand back and forth, from the edge of my shoulder, toward my neck, under my hair and back again and he leaned in closer and looked directly at me. He bit his bottom lip and with the way he was moving his hand back and forth across my back it was so damn sexy I couldn't see straight. I remembered the puppies long enough to decide they really indicated that he was sensitive and sweet.

Then I forgot all about them.

Everything was in slow motion and everything was tingling, radiating out from the spot on the back of my shoulder that he was touching and then he moved his hand up to behind the middle of my neck and pulled me toward him. He put his other hand on my waist for a moment and then it was on my knee and I closed my eyes again and he kissed me really lightly and really softly and then, before I could move, before I could react at all, he pulled away. He put his elbow on the bar and rested his head in his hand and kept his other hand behind my neck and looked at me. "Taking long drives," he said.

I could have stopped playing the game at that point, but one of my absolutely favorite things is to be taken on long drives. I love sitting in the passenger seat of a car and listening to music and looking out the window at whatever scenery is going by. It always makes me feel calm and safe and happy and content. "Going on long drives," I replied, and couldn't have stopped myself from smiling had I wanted to.

"Jane," he said as he put his hand again on the back of my shoulder and looked at me as if I were the only person in the world, "when you get back to New York, I'm going to take you on long drives all the time."

Right before we left the bar he asked about the opening the following night and said he would stop by if that was okay with me; I told him it was. We walked outside and luckily a cab was right there; we both got in and just when I thought nothing could get better, Ryan Dennison went twenty minutes out of his way at one o'clock in the morning to drop me off at my hotel. As soon as we got into the cab he told the driver the name of my hotel and then said, "And then we'll be heading back downtown."

Dreamy was the main word that was floating around in my head as we pulled up to my hotel and Ryan told the driver, "Just a minute," and got out of the cab. He took my hand, helped me out, and said, "I had such a great time and

I'm so glad we met." Then he put his arms around me and hugged me. It was the first time I'd ever gotten hugged good-bye on a date. I didn't know if I was supposed to hug back, or if one hug was good for the both of us. I decided one hug was good for both of us.

"I'll see you tomorrow, Jane. Dabney Gallery on North Michigan, right?"

"Right."

"Okay, then. Bye, Jane Laine. Sleep well." He flashed his kryptonite-coated teeth at me one more time and got into the cab.

27

THANKS FOR DINNER

"I'm really afraid to feel happy
because it never lasts."
—Andy Warhol

From the second I woke up the next morning, as I put the dress I would wear to the opening party into a garment bag and put on jeans and a shirt to get dirty in all day during installation, I couldn't wait for it to be night.

"Cheers, Jane," Ian greeted me as he stood up halfway and I sat down in my customary chair across from him at breakfast in our hotel's lobby café. "How was your evening?" he asked as he cheerily poured me a cup of coffee. "Do I get to hear all about it?"

"Oh, Ian," I gushed. "It was perfect! He's smart and funny," I said, and as I pictured his blond hair and blue eyes, his broad shoulders, I thought how handsome he was, how incredibly attractive. "And he's so pretty," I added. "I know you can't describe men as pretty, but he is, he's darn pretty."

"Sounds lovely, Jane," Ian said, as he looked at me bemusedly.

"You'll get to meet him tonight! He's coming to the opening," I enthusiastically continued.

The eggs Ian had ordered for himself arrived, along with the oatmeal he'd ordered for me. I dreamily ate my breakfast, reliving the previous evening in my mind, until I heard Ian's voice say, "Jane?"

"Yes," I said, back from my reverie.

"All ready to go? Or are you still back having cocktails?" he asked.

"No, all set," I said, warm from my daydreaming. "Let's get going."

I gathered up my bag and we started putting on our coats, gloves, and hats and headed out into the cold.

David Dabney Gallery was the smallest of the galleries we'd exhibited at so far, and setup went by much quicker than it had in London and Rome. There was just one art handler and one staff member present, both clearly already in holiday mode. All the sculptures were small and easily transportable, so it was fine that the two weren't doing anything other than looking at the sculptures, saying they were brilliant, and then wandering off.

Once everything was in place, I sat at the reception desk

and made some changes to the price list and exhibition labels, leaving out what had already been sold at the fair and adding in two new works that had been shipped from New York. The gallery was quiet; the gallery people were out at lunch, and Ian had closeted himself in David Dabney's large office to get some writing done.

I took out my cell and called Kate.

With Kate, I was able to get into all the better details I had left out with Ian. I told her how I felt when he was really close to me, and about the heat that came from his hand on my back.

"Jane," she said when I finally paused, "this guy sounds nice, and it sounds like he is interested in you. Did you call him to thank him?"

"No. I wasn't sure if I should, since I thanked him last night and I'll be seeing him again tonight."

"I say absolutely make the call. He was so polite; he is obviously someone who would appreciate it."

From a manners standpoint, I do believe it is always best to err on the side of politeness. But sometimes a thank-you call can look less like a polite gesture and more like an impatient girl pouncing. It is a fine line, and without much recent experience, I didn't have any reason to believe I'd be good walking it. But Ryan was different; Ryan was a gentleman. "You are absolutely right. I'll call him now."

After Kate and I hung up, I walked into the main gallery and stood in front of *Untitled #17*, soaking up the happiness I was now sure emanated from every Ian Rhys-Fitzsimmons sculpture. Five minutes later, I went back to the phone. I took

Ryan's business card out of my wallet, flipped it over to where he'd written his cell phone number, and dialed.

"Ryan Dennison."

"Ryan. Hi, it's Jane."

"Hiiii, Jane," he sang more than said.

"Hi. How are you?"

"Greeeaaaattt. How are you?"

"I'm good. I wanted to thank you for last night; I had a really nice time," I said.

"It's so nice that you called. Listen," he continued a little less enthusiastically, "everything is a little crazy here. Let me give you a call back when things calm down?"

"Sure," I said. Then I added, "Talk to you later," and was glad I hadn't said, "See you later," even though it was what I was thinking.

"Bye, Jane," he said.

My cell phone rang almost instantly. Things sure had calmed down fast! "Jane Laine," I said plastering a come-hither look on my face, hoping it would come through in my voice.

"Jane, it's Victor . . ."

"Victor! Hi—"

"Listen." He cut me off, whispering loudly, his voice more serious than perhaps I had ever heard it. "Love you, miss you, all that. But I just wanted to warn you, Dick is in an ab-solute rage—" Victor was cut off by the ringing of my land line.

Damn. "Victor, I have to get that. Can you hold?"

"No. I can't. I'll try to call you later. Good luck, honey. Oh, honey. Bye."

I grabbed the other line. "David Dabney Gallery," I said as calmly as possible.

"Jane Laine, please." It was Amanda.

A frantic call from Victor followed immediately by a call from the Velociraptor could be nothing but bad. "Hi, Amanda."

"I'm putting Dick through."

I grabbed onto the desk for support in the interminable second it took to patch Dick through.

"JANE! I just spoke to Peter Brown and he never got any information on *Untitled: Black and Silver.* I SPECIFICALLY remember asking you to do that! WHYDIDN'TYOU?" he screamed.

I, too, specifically remembered him asking me to do it because it was the day he was spelling "BROWN" at me. I also specifically remember him telling me to tell Amanda to do it. Only problem was, right then, with my chest tightening and my heart drumming in fear, I couldn't specifically remember asking Amanda to do it.

"JANE!"

"Uh, Dick?"

"So you have nothing to say for yourself? NOTHING? Nothing!" he said rather triumphantly. "I can't say this isn't exactly the performance I expected!" With that I heard his phone slam down.

I thought briefly about calling him back, and decided it wasn't a feasible option. I replaced my own receiver, knowing that this time he might actually have been justified. "Damn," I said and put my head down on the desk.

• • •

I spent the night looking through the opening as if everything were transparent, as if no one else were there. I also spent the night looking again and again at the door—the door Ryan Dennison never walked through. I tried to tell myself that it didn't matter, that it was one date, one night. That to care too much about a person who was practically a stranger was stupid, would make me a desperate woman clinging to false promises, a woman I'd never, not in a gazillion years, want to be. I told myself it was more important to be upset about other things, about what Dick would do to punish me for my mistake.

I called a taxi, collected my things, and put on my coat, leaving the closing of the gallery and the cleaning up of the opening to the people who worked there. I looked for Ian to see if he needed anything else, because after all, that was why I was there.

"No, but Jane, don't go. Come to dinner, grab a cocktail," he said, and he looked at me with a little bit of concern, but not too much. I could tell he didn't want to make it too obvious that he knew I was upset. Ian walked me to the door and waited with me in silence until the taxi pulled up. I wanted to thank him for always being so considerate of me, and I wanted to thank him for not asking why Ryan didn't show up. Instead I just said good night.

On the way home, it occurred to me that maybe this all felt worse than it should because not having felt this way in a while, I had forgotten how bad it could be. I had forgotten this feeling, this feeling that nothing is good, that everything that seems just fine actually isn't. That really, everything sucks. It was after eleven by the time I put my key card into its slot and opened my hotel room door. I turned on the lights and the TV, then brushed my teeth. My toothbrush felt heavy; when I washed my face, the soap felt like cement.

28

BY GEORGE, I
THINK I'VE GOT IT!

"A person can cry or laugh. Always when you're
crying you could be laughing, you have the
choice. Crazy people know how to do this best
because their minds are loose."
—Andy Warhol

Even with Christmas shining in the distance, no one was buying anything at the gallery. I tried to forget about everything else and focused instead on scrolling through the gallery's client list. I spent my days trolling for patrons who might enjoy being called up by a representative of Dick Reese Gallery so much that they would pop by, fall in love with a sculpture, and buy it. As I concentrated on dialing for dollars, the rest of it stopped seeming so bad.

A week went by and it was Tuesday again, and I remembered that the Art Institute was open late. I thought of the plans that Ian and I had made and wondered if it would have been better if I had never blown him off, never gone out with Ryan at all. Ian walked into the gallery right then, unbuttoning his coat to reveal a bright purple shirt and lilac tie underneath his navy blue suit.

"Hi there, Jane," he said catching his breath as he shivered, still slightly frozen from the lovely Chicago weather.

Hi, clashing shades of purple! "Hey there, Ian. How was your lunch?" I asked. Usually he told me where he was going and who he was going with. This time he hadn't, so I figured he didn't want me to know.

"Good, great. How are things here?"

"Pretty quiet. I spoke to Mr. Sandler and I'm hoping he might be a last-minute Christmas gift purchaser."

"Well, Evelyn Sandler was on the list for #6 so maybe in its absence, a small piece would compensate nicely. Let me know how it goes."

Ian didn't hang around to chat with me, but went into David Dabney's office and stayed there with the door closed for the rest of the afternoon. It seemed as if he had something weighing on his mind and I wondered what it was. I decided it was the perfect night to reschedule our trip to the Art Institute. That should cheer him up.

"Hey, Ian," I said as I knocked on the door. "Are you busy in there?"

"No, just finishing up. Come on in."

I didn't notice any graph paper, nor did I see any of Ian's journals. Seeing him quickly flip his cell phone shut and put it in his pocket, I wondered if he'd been in here talking all afternoon. *Why hadn't he just used the gallery phone?* "It's Tuesday again," I said. "I thought it would be a great night to go to the Art Institute. Since we'll be leaving before the weekend, it's our last chance to go." Or rather, it was my last chance to go. Ian was free to leave the gallery whenever he wanted; I always had to stay. "Or I guess it's our last chance to go together," I added.

"Ah, Jane. That's a lovely idea, but I'm afraid I won't be able to join you. I'm booked up. You should go, though. Say hello to *Sunday Afternoon* for me, will you?"

"Too bad," I said. I felt very disappointed, but tried not to show it. "I'll definitely say hi for you. Have a good night, Ian. See you in the morning,"

"Cheers, Jane. See you at breakfast."

I turned off the computer and walked through the gallery, wondering who Ian had been at lunch with, and who he was going to dinner with, and if they were the same person. Then the gallery door opened and a burst of cold air rushed in.

"Hello zare, Jane."

I looked at her perfect figure draped in tan suede Armani and a dark brown cashmere wrap that made me homesick for Number 5 Maddox Street. I should have known. "Hello, Karina, how are you?"

"Oh you know how it iz," she began and I thought that I, more than likely, didn't know how it waz at all.

"Zee girls at zee gallery, zay book me at zee wrong hotel and zee plane takes off zis morning very early and I am exhausted but had to come to see zee sale at Sudzabees."

I didn't know about any sale at Sotheby's, didn't really

want to know and could not imagine how anyone, even Karina Kratsch, could be on a plane, spend a day at an auction house, possibly breaking to lunch with Ian, and still look as good as she looked.

"Where issss Ian?" she asked and it was as if the mere mention of hisssss name had triggered her breathy mechanism when there had been no breathiness only moments before.

"He's in the office. I'll beep him."

I went by myself to the Art Institute of Chicago. I walked straight to the room where the Seurat was, and sat down on the bench that's right in front of the painting, next to a girl with a sketchpad and a box of colored pencils. I looked at all the dots, stared at different sections, and then looked at the whole scene, everyone with their parasols and elegant clothing, all so relaxed, so peaceful, so free. Then, for a little while, I was with them. I wasn't carrying a laptop and I wasn't wearing a bulky coat, scarf, gloves, and a hat. I was carrying a parasol and wearing a long, petticoated skirt. It wasn't freezing cold outside and I didn't feel lonely at all. I had the company of the beautiful, detailed, perfect people who spent forever on the Island of La Grande Jatte, whose time was always Sunday, and whose season was always summer.

After some time, I looked at the drawing the girl next to me was working on. "That's good," the angel of happiness buried somewhere deep inside me popped up to say.

"Thanks," she answered.

"Have you been working on it long?"

"Well, yes. But just at night. I come here when the museum is open at night."

"That must be a lovely way to spend an evening," I said, thinking of how much safer it would be to spend nights at the museum with Seurat, of how many things could be avoided that way.

"Oh. It is. And you know, sometimes you get to see really cool people. Just last week, you won't believe this, I saw Ian Rhys-Fitzsimmons," she said excitedly.

"Oh, really?"

"He even signed my pad for me. He's the greatest artist there is." She turned to a page in her pad that Ian had written his name across and I thought of him being embarrassed by such a request but, never wanting to be rude, complying with it all the same.

"Wow," I told her, admiring the prized signature along with her.

"He was unhappy, though."

"Unhappy?"

"Yeah. He just sat in front of the painting all night looking very sad."

As I walked into my room and turned to the salad section of the room service menu, I sighed.

I ordered my salad and then thought I'd check my e-mail. There weren't any, probably because so many people were off to wherever they were spending Christmas and New Year's Eve. Ugh. New Year's Eve. New Year's Eve isn't anyone's favorite night. I'm sure of it. The weather is always horrible and you can't ever get a cab and it is just a big pain. And it's never any fun if you are single.

I didn't sign off right then.

I was remembering an e-mail I'd barely glanced at, way back when.

I started scrolling through days and days of e-mails. *London*, I thought. *Late October*. There it was. Unlike most other e-mails in my inbox, there was no flippy arrow to its left because—rather rudely—I had never replied.

Mail to: planejane6@hotmail.com
From: George.Oreganato@feldenandkamer.com
Re: Santa Fe

Jane,

Nice to see you last night, as always. Hope you enjoy the rest of your time here and at the other stops on your tour. I realize it's a bit far away but since you mentioned you'd be in Santa Fe for the Art Dealers Federation Fair, I assume you'll be there for New Year's Eve. I'm thinking of organizing a dinner for about six people—various friends/associates who will be there for the fair. Should you find yourself free that night, I'd love it if you would join us.

Bon voyage,
George Oreganato

And then, just like that, it hit me. Wouldn't it be so much easier and so much less painful to have a boyfriend just like

George? Is finding someone who makes your stomach flip really so important? Are fabulous first kisses and romance really even necessary in the long run? First kisses become second ones and third ones and stop being so fabulous anyway. And love, is that really as important as never having to wonder whether someone is going to call you? As important as never again having to wonder if you'll be alone forever?

I thought how, very possibly, it wasn't.

Maybe that's exactly what I needed to accept.

Mail to: George.Oreganato@feldenandkamer.com

From: planejane6@hotmail.com

RE: Re: Santa Fe

Dear George,

I'm so sorry it has taken me this long to get back to you. Thanks so much for the invitation for New Year's Eve. If the offer still stands, and if you're not already spoken for, I would love to join you for dinner. Hope all is going well with you.

All best,

Jane

29

GUESS WHO'S COMING
TO DINNER?

"Everybody will be famous for 15 minutes."
—Andy Warhol

Art Dealers Federation Fair
Santa Fe, New Mexico

"How many hours to Santa Fe?" Ian asked me as we walked toward baggage claim in the Albuquerque airport. There was a look of anticipation on his face; his zeal for travel had not been satisfied by the four-hour flight from Chicago, and the additional hour we had spent waiting on the runway there.

"I think the drive's about an hour, hour and a half."

No one in the world loves traveling more than Ian. It wasn't until we were waiting for our rental car that it occurred to me that he hadn't gone anywhere for Christmas.

We were standing in the Albuquerque airport together, and it was Christmas Eve.

"Ian, how come you didn't go home for Christmas?" I asked, hoping he didn't think I was as completely, vilely self-centered as I felt for only just then inquiring.

"No, not this year, no."

"Why not?"

"Well, there's been so much traveling and I hate flying and I got to see my family a lot in October. I thought it better this year, with the project and all, just to stay in the States."

What? My mouth dropped open. "But you love flying."

He paused and I saw a flash of something in his eyes. "Right, yes," he said, smiling awkwardly, slightly off, slightly weird. "I do, indeed. Just a lot of work to do, is all."

"Do you have plans for tonight? For tomorrow?" I asked, not wanting to think of him sitting in Santa Fe eating a Christmas enchilada by himself.

"Yes, yes. I've got plans tonight." *With the PR bimbi, perhaps?* "And tomorrow a yoga ashram outside of town is having a sweat lodge."

"A sweat lodge?"

"Yes, it is a Native American ceremony. Supposed to be very spiritually and emotionally cleansing. They have one on Christmas Day and one on New Year's Day. I've never tried it and have always wanted to. After that, I'm going to catch up on some writing. I didn't get very much done last week."

I wondered again what it was that had been preoccupying him these last few days and what, if anything, it had to do with Karina Kratsch's mysterious visit. Maybe whichever PR bimbo he dated had said he had to choose between her and

Karina? Maybe he'd had to select from blond, blonder, or blondest? "Come with me for Christmas, then," I said, sure he wouldn't want to, sure he'd say, "No, thank you." Sure, too, that I wouldn't have to explain about Elijah the Schnauzer being here, visiting family, and sure I wouldn't ever have to tell him about the paper hats my Dad insists everyone wear at Christmas.

"Oh, I'd love that," he said, smiling. "Are you sure it won't be an imposition?"

"No, no, none at all," I said, trying to smile, too.

"Brilliant!" he said as the rental car person handed him our keys.

About an hour later, Ian pulled up to La Posada, the hotel we'd be staying at for the month. I could see a cluster of adobe cottages sprawled out behind the main building and the air was crisp. Inside, a fire was burning somewhere and the smell made me think of coming into a ski lodge after being on the slopes all day. The house my parents had rented was just up the road. Ian didn't need the car, so I took it. I gave him the address of my parents' rented house and we made plans for him to come over the next day at three. If anything changed, we'd call each other.

"Merry Christmas Eve, Ian. See you tomorrow."

"Cheers, Jane. See you then."

As I pulled out of the hotel driveway, I looked at the digital display on the car's clock. Five o'clock. Plenty of time to be home for dinner, to hope that Elijah had already been to visit her family, plenty of time to fill Mom in on the fact that

we'd be having Ian over for dinner tomorrow. I mentally
ticked off the members of my family and tried to determine
who would and would not be able to deal with someone as
famous as Ian. My dad would be fine; Mom I wasn't so sure
about. Nana and Uncle Fred I thought would probably em-
barrass me, and I was sure there wasn't any way that Aunt
Sandy, who was herself an artist, would be able to keep it together. No way.

Elijah, of course, wouldn't care at all.

I pulled up to the curb, parked, and headed up the short
walk to the house. Mom had left a note on the door. Mom,
Dad, Nana, Aunt Sandy, and Uncle Fred had all gone with
Elijah up to Taos to visit her family. They planned to be back
by six. That gave me just enough time before everyone got
home to unpack a few things and to plug in my laptop to check
my e-mail.

Mail to: planejane6@hotmail.com

From: George.Oreganato@feldenandkamer.com

RE: Re: Re: Santa Fe

Hi Jane, so nice to hear from you. Thrilled you will be joining us
for New Year's Eve. I'll get the details to you, closer to the date.
I hope that all is going well with you and look forward to seeing
you.

Happy Holidays,
George Oreganato
P.S. No, not spoken for ☺

Perfect.

30

PASS THE SCHNAUZER ON THE
LEFT-HAND SIDE

"Being born is like being kidnapped.
And then sold into slavery."
—Andy Warhol

The people who have Elijah's puppy had not, to my mother's disappointment, invited our entire family over for Christmas. They thought she was insane. So it was just me and my parents, Nana and Uncle Fred, and Aunt Sandy and Elijah. We all enjoyed a leisurely Christmas morning. Except for Elijah, who was dashing around, checking out room after room and then starting over.

Ian arrived at three, with a beautiful pottery vase for my mom.

After introductions were made, some wine was opened, and even with my aunt getting a little hysterical telling Ian what an influence he had on her own artwork, everyone got along really well. Mom had been agreeable about Elijah not eating from the table, and even though Dad wouldn't budge on the paper hats, as we headed into the dining room for dinner I was happy Ian was with us.

Then I stopped short. In between my mom's place setting and the place setting labeled *Ian* was a setting that said, simply, *Elijah*. Lots of families leave room for Elijah at their dinner tables. But they are celebrating Passover! There aren't usually places marked 'Elijah' at tables where a family of lapsed Lutherans will celebrate Christmas. The place setting that stopped me short wasn't a long-practiced religious tradition. It was a place setting for a Schnauzer with an eating disorder.

"*Mo-om*," I said in the loudest whisper I could manage, clenching my teeth and darting my eyes, trying to be as subtle as I could.

"Ja-ane," Mom mimicked me, clenching her own teeth and rolling her eyes and not making any attempt to be subtle at all.

As Ian stood properly behind his chair, and Elijah jumped on to the chair next to him, I realized the mistake I'd made. I'd forgotten to cover all my bases. In the happiness and relief I'd felt when Mom had agreed that Elijah wouldn't eat at the table, I'd forgotten to make sure that "not eating at table" also encompassed not sitting there.

We all sat down and opened up our paper Christmas crackers.

All except for Elijah—her cracker was opened by Mom.

Inside the crackers were the paper crowns in different colors. Bright pointy crowns in pink, purple, yellow, green, and blue popped up around the table, reminding me very much of one of Ian's shirts. As we all, except for Elijah, got up to fill our plates at the buffet table, Ian was smiling happily in a hot pink paper crown. As if it were all the most normal thing in the world—everyone wearing paper hats, a dog sitting at the table with her very own place setting.

Sitting back down, I noticed Mom was sitting quietly with her hands in her lap and staring at the empty plate in front of her. I worried where that was going. Was she not going to eat, in protest of Elijah's not being allowed to eat at the table?

"What do you do?" Nana asked, focusing on Ian with an intense stare.

"I'm an artist," Ian told her, pleased to have been asked this question that probably no one ever asked.

"Janie likes art. Janie works in a gallery for a horrible man."

"Yes," Ian said and winked across the table at me.

"What kind of an artist?" Nana continued.

"I'm a sculptor."

"Not very much money in that." Nana made a little *humph* sound, after which she reached over and patted Ian's hand. "Don't worry, dear. You're young, you'll figure out something to do." With that she picked up her fork and knife and focused on her roast. I started breathing again, glad the conversation was over, and started on my own dinner.

"Are you Lutheran?" Nana asked.

"Pardon?" said Ian after hastily chewing his first taste of his dinner.

"Are you Lutheran?"

"Nana—" I started. I looked over helplessly at my father, but he was busily eating, wearing his paper crown almost as proudly as Ian was wearing his.

"Oh, no. Not Lutheran," he told her.

"Catholic? So many problems in your church now. It must be terrible for you."

"Well, no. I'm not Catholic. Church of England, actually."

"Never heard of it," Nana said, waving her hand as if it didn't exist. I wondered how we'd gotten onto religion when I heard her say, "Well, dear, maybe you could become Lutheran. I would like that much better. Seems Janie never dates Lutherans. What was that last one? From Texas? The Methodist? Never much liked him anyway. And I was right, wasn't I? No sense of honor, that one."

"Nana, really, um—" I started to say.

"Oh, Janie, shush. Ian and I are having a nice conversation."

I looked over at Ian. I tried to catch his eye to let him know that I was sorry, that I was mortified, that I was adopted, but he didn't look toward me. He was completely focused on Nana, waiting intently for her next words.

"Too tall also. No reason for anyone to be as tall as that one was," she explained to everyone before focusing her attention completely on Ian again. "You aren't tall at all. You're actually too short. But that's probably better for Jane. She's a bit of a shrimp herself."

"Nana," I seized a moment of silence, "Ian and I aren't

dating. We work together. We're friends." I could feel myself blushing and when I looked up again Ian was looking at me. He smiled and just in the way his eyes held mine and the way his expression changed, he seemed somehow to be saying that everything was fine, that everything was in fact, lovely.

"Oh," said Nana, looking bewildered for a moment. Then in a loud whisper, she said, "Just as well. Nice as he seems, there's no money and those Catholics, they like a million kids running all over the place and with you being no spring chicken, you don't have the time left to have a million kids."

"No! Not a spring chicken, that's for sure!" added Uncle Fred.

"Yes, not quite a spring chicken," agreed Aunt Sandy.

"You'll always be a spring chicken to me," said my dad. *Thanks, Dad.*

I busied myself with an intense study of the floor. I was concentrating so intently that when the howling started, it took me a minute to realize what it was. Right next to Ian, Elijah had her nose pointed to the ceiling and was letting out a deep, soulful howl.

No, Elijah. Please, no!

"What is it, Elijah?" Aunt Sandy asked loudly, straining to be heard over the noise. And I knew it was coming. I knew Mom wouldn't be able to refrain from this opportunity. I knew this just as surely as I knew there was nothing I could do to stop it. I threw one last imploring glance at my mother, hoping against hope she might pick that very moment to test out dog food and a dog bowl.

"Elijah, poor thing, must be hungry," she said to my aunt. Then turning to Ian, she added loudly, "Jane doesn't want Elijah to eat at the table since you're here and I promised her she wouldn't."

Ian was pressing his lips together. I was sure any second he would run screaming into the street, an idea that was looking increasingly attractive to me as each yowling second passed. Miraculously, he pulled himself together and smiled kindly at my mother.

"Please don't let her suffer needlessly on my account."

Elijah stopped howling and hung her head in shame in front of her plate. Maybe it was because she looked so sad and devastated sitting there . . . or maybe it was the only way to stop Mom from explaining all of Elijah's eating disorders, and her self-esteem issues, and third therapist. And after all, it was Christmas. I said, "It's fine, Mom. Elijah needs to eat."

In a show of good sportsmanship, I got up from the table and went into the kitchen. There, exactly where I thought it would be, waiting right in the middle of the kitchen table, was a plate of puréed roast beef, blended green beans, and mashed potatoes. I took a deep breath, tried to accept who I was, and walked back into the dining room to present Elijah with her Christmas dinner.

Everyone went back to their own dinners, Mom got busy making spoon airplanes for Elijah, and we didn't talk anymore about religion or Ian not making any money and everything seemed okay.

"Is it time?" Aunt Sandy asked just as everyone was finishing up coffee and cake.

Damn you, Aunt Sandy.

"Oh, I think it is!" said Mom, clapping her hands.

Damn me for not remembering.

"Pass the Schnauzer!" exclaimed Dad. *Dad! No!*

"Pass her indeed!" boomed Uncle Fred.

They all started clapping rhythmically together, swaying from side to side. Ian looked at me for guidance. But I had none; I had no advice to give him on how to behave. Mortified, I just stared at him and shook my head. He smiled at me, shrugged, and began clapping along. The only choices left to me seemed to be going into the kitchen and putting my head in the oven or clapping with everyone else. Surprising, I know, but I chose clapping. We all clapped and swayed; Elijah barked occasionally. Then the clapping slowed and finally stopped. Everyone looked expectantly at Ian. I closed my eyes.

"Ian," Nana said, sounding more than a little exasperated. "Elijah is always passed to the left."

"Passed?" he queried.

"Yes, pass her to me. To the left," Nana said impatiently.

"Ah, okay. And she won't mind if I pick her up?" Ian gingerly reached over to Elijah's chair and put his hands on either side of her.

"No, no, of course not. That's. The. Whole. Point."

He looked helplessly in my direction, and then, with a grin, picked up Elijah, who wiggled and squirmed a little but was generally agreeable. Everyone resumed their clapping and Ian looked expectantly at Nana as he held Elijah out toward her.

"She has to KISS you first!" hollered Uncle Fred.

Damn you, Uncle Fred!

Ian hesitated for just a second and then obliged, leaning

his face toward Elijah. She frantically slobbered wet licks all over his face and a lot of his neck. Elijah made her way around the table, kissing everyone, showered with praise and cries of "Good girl!" as she went.

I tried to be happy Dad hadn't put on the Yaz *Upstairs at Eric's* CD, blaring the song "Situation"—the one where Alison Moyet keeps saying "Move out!"—from the stereo. How that specific song became the theme song of Pass the Schnauzer is as hard to remember as how the game itself actually came into existence. I tried to find solace in the fact that even though we were clapping and swaying and passing our dog around the table, at least we weren't all moving to a disco-techno beat.

Then I looked over at Elijah, slathering kisses all over my mother's neck, her journey complete. Everyone was still clapping and Elijah stopped kissing and looked out at the table, wiggling her bottom around in rhythmic opposition to the ecstatic jerks of her head. And the thing was, she looked happy. *Really,* really happy. Her eyes glistened and she wiggled around so thrilled, and her face looked exactly as if she were smiling. Elijah, who had struggled for years with what her second therapist called doggie depression, had faced her demons. And although it included baby food and sitting at the table and being passed around it, Elijah had figured it out.

After a bit longer at the table, Ian helped me clear the plates.

Although I'd been with him constantly for months, and although we had become friends, there was still something a little bit surreal about having the greatest artist of all time standing in the kitchen next to me, scraping puréed roast beef off a plate.

We joined everyone in the living room and Mom told Ian how the people who had bought Elijah's puppy were really quite ungracious. Not only didn't they invite us for dinner, they didn't seem to want to spend any time with Elijah. Just as well, she explained, since everyone was heading back to New York the next day. Nana thought maybe Ian could go into accounting and he agreed wholeheartedly. He also agreed to seriously look into converting to Lutheran when she brought that up again.

"I'm glad you came," I told him as we stood alone at the front door an hour later.

"I am, too. Your family is lovely."

"Thanks."

"Thank you for inviting me."

"Sure." I couldn't help smiling, marveling at the absence of any need to make apologies. "I'll see you in the morning."

He didn't say anything for a long minute. I saw his eyes change from looking like he was about to say something, to just warm and smiling. Then something happened—my stomach tightened up, flipping over. Ian leaned in and kissed me on the cheek. Zig. Zag. I kept my eyes closed because I didn't want to look at him. What on earth was I thinking? *This is Ian,* I said to myself, and opened my eyes. I thought, *If George Oreganato and I wind up together, I'll never have this feeling again.*

"Thanks again."

"You're welcome." The act of speaking scared away the

zigzag feeling. I tried to smile and forget it all and act as if I were a normal person.

Ian walked down the path that led from the front door and I watched him walk away and turn the corner. I stayed there for a long while, in the doorway of the adobe house, concentrating on the empty space that had been filled with Ian.

31

HAPPY NEW YEAR

"As soon as you stop wanting
something, you get it."
—Andy Warhol

Mail to: planejane6@hotmail.com

From: George.Oreganato@feldenandkamer.com

Hi, Jane. Meeting time tonight is between 9:00 and 9:30 at
Geronimo's. It's on Canyon Road. See you there.

George Oreganato

Santa Fe was beautiful. The air was crisp and it was really
true—the light there was different from anywhere else in the
world. The weather was warm and it was like springtime
every day. A positive, festive energy filled the Art Dealers
Federation Fair. Three days after the opening of the fair, I was

fairly certain Ian's girlfriend was the less blond, less thin bimbo. She came to our booth a lot more times than the other one.

Setting up and organizing, passing out press releases at previews, and getting ready for openings had all become second nature. It was great how used to the process we had become, but sad, too, because next month the Miami Art Fair was the last stop. It didn't seem like it was time for the Art Fair Project to be over. But I was really looking forward to being back in New York for two weeks, and then an entire month in Miami. It would be so wonderful to see Kate whenever I wanted, just like before she and Diego moved away. I had a lot to look forward to, not least of all New Year's Eve.

And my date with George Oreganato.

I left the hotel that night at nine o'clock wearing my new turquoise necklace and a black sweater and skirt. I breathed in the fresh crisp air, thinking once more how good it was to be warm again. I walked past the galleries that lined Canyon Road: contemporary art, southwestern art, American art, and tourist art all living snugly together in little houses, broken up every few buildings by alternately cute and festive restaurants and cafés.

Canyon Road seems a lot friendlier and much less competitive than all the huge hangarlike spaces that fill the blocks in Chelsea. I thought maybe after I lived in Rome, if I ever needed to come back to the States, I'd move to Santa Fe. I'd be noncompetitive and nonconfrontational, and I'd go to yoga classes all the time and eat salsa and wear turquoise and live in an adobe house. I could even start painting, inspired by the landscape and the light. Maybe I would be the next Georgia O'Keeffe, and there would be a Jane Laine museum right in town that art lovers from around the world would flock to.

I arrived at Geronimo's with a blister on my toe from walking in high-heeled slingbacks. George was sitting at a table with, as he had said, six other people. I didn't recognize any of them. I felt a pang of nervousness and wondered if this really was the best way to spend New Year's Eve. Then George saw me and raised his arm to be sure I noticed him and smiled at me. And even though his teeth were very big, as I got closer to him, I noticed that they were also very straight and very white.

"Jane. Hi! Everyone, this is my friend Jane Laine and Jane Laine, this is everyone," he said, chuckling. "This is," he continued gesturing to each couple as he said their names, "Lance and Joanna. And Sarah and Alex. And here, we have Meredith and Michael."

Lance, Joanna, Sarah, Alex, Meredith, and Michael all said hello and checked me out, and I said hello right back at them. Everyone was very pleasant, and no one was any more dressed up than I was. Sarah and Alex were clients of George's gallery and in town for the art fair; Meredith and Michael lived in Santa Fe and seemed to know Sarah and Alex very well. Joanna and Lance were staying in Taos and talked a lot about skiing. Even though Sarah and Alex got all excited because I knew Ian Rhys-Fitzsimmons, it turned out to be a much less business-oriented dinner than I had thought it would be. We didn't talk about art or art fairs or any of it, and it was a welcome change. I had been living, breathing, eating, and drinking the art world, and it was good to get away from it. During dinner Joanna asked George something about carpentry, and then Sarah jumped in praising a window bench George had built for her. I thought how nice it was that George was handy, and suddenly he seemed a lot less Barbie.

We all drank champagne and by the time it was almost midnight, I'd forgotten that not so long ago, all I'd wanted from George was for him to go away. I was very much enjoying being a couple among other couples. As everyone in the restaurant started yelling, "Ten," I thought how it would be so easy to be part of a couple with George.

"Nine!" We work in the same field, so we'll always have that in common.

"Eight!" I've never heard him mention football or baseball so maybe he doesn't like them and we can do things on Sundays other than watch televised sporting events.

"Seven!" He never talks about golf.

"Six!" He is handy; he can build things. There is something very attractive about a man who can install your kitchen floor, should you need that.

"Five!" He is tall.

"Four!" There is no reason why, after a while, I can't subtly mention that argyle socks are geeky and maybe he shouldn't wear them.

"Three!" His teeth aren't that big.

"Two!" Jane Oreganato has a certain international ring to it, doesn't it?

"One!" And he likes me.

Everyone started kissing each other and I turned and smiled at George, thinking that this New Year's hadn't turned out so badly at all. Then George just kept looking at me and it was me and George staring at each other, not kissing, in the midst of this vast sea of everyone kissing and saying, "Happy New Year."

Everyone was singing along with the New Year's Eve song and George still hadn't kissed me. I finished what could very well have been my millionth glass of champagne and leaned over to kiss him. He didn't kiss me back. As I collided with all those teeth, it occurred to me that this could well be his revenge for my not kissing him in London and caring only about Owen Wilson.

"Jane," he said as I sat back and smiled at him feebly, "do you want to go outside and have a cigarette?"

"But you don't smoke."

"But you do," he observed. It would take too many words to explain my smoking situation, so I just nodded and followed him.

"Look," he said as we got outside, "I'm drawing a complete blank."

"What?"

"Jane, this is the first time anything like this has ever happened to me." He seemed bewildered. "I'm not sure what's going on but, it's just, I look at you and it's a complete blank. I mean, in London, yes, I was so into you. I thought about you all the time. But now, I guess, I'm just over it."

"What?"

"I hope we can still be friends."

In London he was into me? What about all the years before? What about all the years and years? And this is the only time something like this has happened to him? I was the only person he had kissed who had caused him to draw a complete blank? That definitely didn't make me feel any better. But then, I couldn't quite believe that any part of what he said was really aimed at making me feel better.

"Okay," I said and wished for cigarettes to fall from the sky along with the time-travel machine I'd been waiting an eternity for.

We got back to the table and George was soon busy talking with Alex about something at the art fair, and everyone else was involved in their own separate conversations. I knew I should have said good-bye to Sarah and Alex and Meredith and Michael and the skiing couple whose names I couldn't remember anymore. And I knew I should have offered George some money for the bill, since we were just friends and not on any sort of date. I knew I should have done all those things, but as I headed toward the door, I don't know what happened. I guess I just drew a complete blank.

Walking home that night, back down Canyon Road, my feet were hurting much more than they did on the way there. I took off my shoes and walked along barefoot, my feet turning the same orange shade as the dust on the ground. I realized that after I had decided that George Oreganato was the answer to everything, I had forgotten to make any New Year's resolutions.

32

WHERE'S IAN?

*"I wonder if it's possible to have
a love affair that lasts forever."*
—Andy Warhol

I tried to clear all memories of the night before out of my head. It was a new year. I had the day off in beautiful Santa Fe and I knew *exactly* what I wanted to do. I wanted to go to Ten Thousand Waves.

I'd been looking at a brochure recommending it that was left in my hotel room. It was a beautiful spa up in the mountains. Very Zen. Very cleansing for the New Year. Very Perfect. I called, and, miracle of miracles, they had a slot open. I scheduled a massage and an all-over body salt scrub. I thought I'd go over early to sit in one of their many special tubs. I hurried to the bathroom to brush my teeth. I was so excited about my salt exfoliation that I almost didn't hear the knock on the door.

I opened it and standing out front was Ian, in orange shorts and some sort of Hawaiian shirt, black sunglasses on in place of his usual frames.

"Cheers, Jane! Happy New Year," he said brightly.

"Cheers yourself. Happy New Year, too."

"What are you doing today?"

"Don't be too jealous. I'm going to the Ten Thousand Waves spa. Very Zen. Very fabulous."

"I came to make sure you didn't want to go to the sweat lodge. Probably not fabulous, as you say, but definitely very Zen."

"No way," I told him without a second's consideration.

"Come on. It'll be fun. It'll be different."

I opened my mouth to tell him to ditch the whole ridiculous sweat lodge thing and to come to Ten Thousand Waves with me. Then I remembered how he'd said he'd always wanted to do it, and how he'd planned on going on Christmas Day. He was always so agreeable and so polite, I worried that if I were to invite him, he might indeed change his plans. I didn't want him to miss out on an experience he'd so been looking forward to. I closed my mouth, thinking, *Different can be good, different can be fun.* I told him to hold on a minute while I canceled my appointment at Ten Thousand Waves.

I had pictured a wooden, Lincoln-log-type house. Or in the absence of that, I thought there would be a large, adobe-type structure. I didn't think either of those assumptions to be unreasonable given the name "sweat *lodge*." *Lodge* means a large houselike structure. Was I really so off base to think we were just going to lie in a cabin on a pair of chaises while a few yoga enthusiasts preformed some sort of cleansing ritual near us?

However, the sweat "lodge" in actuality was not a lodge at all.

As Ian and I got out of our car and walked over a hill, I saw a metal framework set up much in the shape of an igloo. Over this framework, people in bathing suits were hanging a tremendous number of heavy wool blankets until it was a tiny igloo completely covered in wool. Then I saw men taking large pieces of rock from the middle of this huge fire right next to the sweat igloo and carrying them inside. The rocks were glowing orange. I wondered how hot they had to be in order to be glowing like that.

About forty people were lined up outside the wool-blanket lodge; certainly there wasn't any way they were all going to fit inside? Ian and I took everything off but our bathing suits and joined the end of the line. Like magic, all the people in front of us went into the lodge. As Ian and I approached, it dawned on me that we were going in there, too.

"Are you ready?" asked a woman wearing a brown robe and feather-themed jewelry.

"Yes," we both said, Ian's "Yes" greatly more enthusiastic.

As she motioned for me to stand with my legs spread and arms out to the side she passed what seemed to be a smoldering candle—she called it a smudge pot—all around us. "There are four doors in the sweat lodge," she explained. "North, South, East, West. We will devote twenty minutes to each door. Concentrate now on what you would like to leave behind in the sweat lodge. The goal is to leave behind that which no longer serves you and that which you will live better without."

I didn't concentrate on what I needed to leave behind; I thought instead how at Ten Thousand Waves they had something called Watsu. They put you in a pool with a floaty noodle and someone swirls you lovingly around as if you are in a water ballet. The swami lady pulled back the blanket and Ian walked into the darkness. I took a deep breath and walked in after him.

People moved around a little bit and I found a seat among a sea of sweating slippery bodies and wondered where Ian was. The swami shut the blanket and then everything was pitch black except for the faintest orange glowing of the rocks in the middle. Within seconds, I was engulfed in more heat than I ever thought I could tolerate. The swami was speaking but I couldn't hear anything. We were one minute into an eighty-minute stretch and I had to leave right that very second. My heart was racing and my throat was closing. I was milliseconds away from crawling over all the people in a desperate rush for the blanket door. Then someone started to talk.

"It's only temporary," I heard. "Just be peaceful and remember that it won't feel like this forever. It won't be like this for long. Remember again that no feeling is permanent and remember all the benefits you will receive for getting through this."

I wasn't sure who said it, and I wasn't sure what the benefits were going to be, but remembering that all this misery was temporary made it a little easier to stick with, to muddle through. I felt like there was a purpose. One I couldn't see yet. Then people started chanting and all I felt was hot.

I tried to concentrate on the chanting and to ignore the sweat of other people dripping onto me. I tried not to listen to the people moaning on either side of me. Every time the swami lady hit her drum, all I could think was, how long had it been since she had done it before? Some freak next to me was laughing. Why was he laughing? It was so fucking hot I felt as if my face were going to melt off. I was sure my bathing suit was going to burst into flame. I had to get it off. I had to get it off! The swami lady poured water onto the stones and there was absolutely no way that I could live inside my bathing suit for one second longer. There in the pitch darkness, with other people sweating all over me, I pulled down the top. Oh, that was better. That was nice. That was better. No, it wasn't. For like half a second, maybe, but now it was bad again. *Real bad. Really, really bad.* I was suffocating. I was going to die. Oh, God, and the moaning. It was the moaning that was going to kill me long before the suffocating.

It was only getting hotter. It had to be over. When would it be over? It was never going to be over. I tried to remember what the swami lady said the point was. What the MOTHERFUCKING FUCK was the point? It was to leave something, to leave something you no longer needed behind. Do it, I thought. *DO IT NOW! Whatever needs to be left here, just leave it! NOW!*

"Sisters. Brothers. Children. Look to the West and look to your ancestors for strength. If you chant, the strength will come to you," sang the swami lady and, oh my God, I couldn't believe it, she just poured more water on the rocks. But she'd said *West*. West was last, right? North, South, East, West. She had said *West*. She had! Then she started chanting, "*Ganesha om namonarayana.*" And then all the moaning people stopped moaning and started repeating after her.

"*Om namonarayana. Om namonarayana. Om namonarayana.*"

I had no idea what it meant, but short of standing up and screaming, "Let me out of here, you lunatic hippies," I felt that chanting with them was my only means of survival.

"*Om namonarayana,*" I said softly.

Then I said it again louder. "*Om namonarayana.*" I closed my eyes and swayed in rhythm with the liquid guy who was swaying next to me. "*Om namonarayana,*" I sang as loud as I could and thought how the last twenty minutes must almost be up. I thought how it was a good thing that no one had a camera with a powerful flash. I started to laugh, picturing myself sitting in the lotus position inside a teepee made of wool blankets, drenched with sweat, eyes closed, swaying and chanting.

Then the door opened and I scrambled to get out of there.

I crawled on all fours out of the sweat lodge and kept going, trying to get as far away from the blanketed structure as possible. I didn't know where Ian was. *Where is Ian? Where is he?* What I wanted most of all was to find Ian. I had to find Ian. As best as I could from my vantage point on all fours, I scanned around and tried desperately to find him, looking at all the people crouching, slumping over, lying flat on their faces. I knew then that I had been looking for Ian for a very long time.

I knew that I had been looking for Ian forever.

I had spent a lifetime looking for the perfect man; I'd always thought he'd be tall and athletic and all-American. I'd thought he'd watch football and play golf and go drinking with the boys. And it wasn't that I wanted any of those things, it was just that for some reason I thought that was how he should be. But that was all completely wrong. The man that I was looking for didn't need to be tall or Texan or any of the rest of it. The man that I was looking for only needed to be one thing. He only needed to be Ian.

Ian was good to me. He treated me with respect. He made me laugh and he made me happy. He was brilliant and dedicated and meaningful. I'd been so busy enjoying our conversations that I hadn't paid attention to the fact that I'd been, all along, falling in love with him. I'd been looking for him my whole life, but it wasn't until that moment, in the middle of the desert, that I knew I had found him.

I had to get to him. I had to tell him.

But first, I had to get up. It might be easier if I stood on my knees rather than trying to go right to my feet. I sat with my legs folded underneath me and slowly took my hands off of the ground. That really seemed to be as far as I could get right then. I looked around at all the other people lying on the ground. I began crawling again, as clearly, walking was not going to be an option. As I traveled forward slowly, I wondered if maybe my news might be better received if I wasn't red-faced and drowned in sweat? Maybe I shouldn't be cross-eyed when making my declaration of love? *But love waits not for beauty!* What? *Om.*

"*Om,*" I repeated again and again trying to remember what came after it.

"Jane? Jane, are you okay?" I heard somewhere, far away off in the distance. Or right next to me, I couldn't be sure

And then there he was. There was sweaty, red-faced, drowned in his own sweat and the sweat of others, Ian. I looked up at him thinking he was the most beautiful thing I had ever seen. I wondered how much time had passed, if somewhere during my journey, I had stopped my forward motion and had remained in one spot, on my hands and knees, chanting *Om.* Or if it just seemed like that had happened.

"Jane, here let me help you up," he said and leaned over and helped me to my feet.

"Ian." I looked at him and thought, *I found you.*

"Have you had any water?" he asked.

"No."

"Well, you've got to. Here, drink this." He handed me a big bottle of water. I held the bottle in front of me and stared at it, thinking it was surely the most beautiful thing I had ever seen. "Water." I looked at it and thought, *I found you, too.* Then I started drinking and I felt so much better. I couldn't stop; it was so good. *So good.* Finally, I was able to take it away from my mouth and hand it back. I looked right at him and didn't even bother taking a deep breath for bravery, because taking small breaths was still very challenging. Out of the corner of my eye, I could see people forming a circle around the fire. *There is more ceremony? Will I still be spiritually cleansed if I skip this part?* I desperately needed to tell Ian how I felt. But then, looking up at him, I suddenly felt overwhelmingly nauseated. He looked down at me and I looked down, too. I was topless.

And then there were two Ians and everything was spinning slowly and then everything was spinning faster. Ian saying "Jane" was the last thing I heard as my knees collapsed underneath me and I fell to the ground. I threw up on his feet right before I passed out.

33

IF ANDY WARHOL
HAD A GIRLFRIEND

"The most exciting thing is not-doing-it.
If you fall in love with someone and
never do it, it's much more exciting."
—Andy Warhol

Fortunately, thankfully, the remaining days of the Santa Fe fair were very busy. All of our sculptures sold and we had to have three smaller sculptures shipped out to us. There were many more cocktail parties and events than there had been in Chicago and luckily, I saw George Oreganato at only one of them. It was good to be busy all day, back at parties each night, drinking champagne and eating cheese sticks. It left a lot less time to be alone with Ian. I wished the only reason I didn't want to be alone with him was because I was embarrassed about being topless in front of him and throwing up on him. But the truth was, it got a lot harder to be with Ian after I knew I was in love with him.

During the weeklong exhibit we had in town at the Big Possum gallery and while Ian was in Galisteo working on a sculpture, I spent a lot of time thinking about an internship I had at the Whitney Museum.

Part of my job was to give museum tours if one of the regular docents was busy. After the sweat lodge, I thought again and again about one day in particular. I'd just given a tour to a group of second-graders. As we stood on the first floor of the museum, right by the elevators, in front of Andy Warhol's *Campbell's Soup Cans,* I asked if there were any questions.

"Did Andy Warhol have a girlfriend?" asked a small girl.

"I'm sorry?" I said.

"Did Andy Warhol have a girlfriend?" she asked again, the children in front of her moving away as she came closer to me.

"Um, no," I said, "he didn't."

"Why not?" she asked.

"He just didn't?" I said, and looked desperately for another little hand to pop up, so I could call on it and answer a different question. But no little hands popped up.

"But why not?" she asked again.

I didn't think I could say that Andy Warhol didn't have a girlfriend because he had a boyfriend. "It just wasn't meant to be," I told her, hoping that would be enough.

"No?" she asked.

"No," I said again. "Some things just aren't meant to be."

"But it sure would have been neat if he did," she told me.

"Absolutely," I agreed, "it would have been neat if he did."

After the sweat lodge, whenever I looked at Ian I'd have to remind myself of that. *Some things just aren't meant to be.* No matter how neat it would be if they were. Ian was my friend. Ian was the best person I'd met in my whole life. I didn't want to tell him I had more than feelings of friendship for him and have him say, "Oh, Jane. I'm so sorry but I don't feel that way at all. I am so sorry if I have ever given you the wrong idea." I didn't want that. I didn't want anything to happen that would make it so that Ian wasn't any longer my friend, so that he wasn't the best person I'd ever met in my whole life.

Every day I tried to put what I felt out of my mind.

Just as I told the little girl who asked me if Andy Warhol had a girlfriend, I had to tell myself that some things just aren't meant to be. As I packed up sculptures and prepared for our return to New York, I thought it would be okay if I never told him how I felt. Just knowing that I loved him was enough.

34

MAYBE LATER

> "Sometimes people let the same
> problem make them miserable for years when
> they could just say, 'so what.' That's one of my
> favorite things to say. 'So what.'"
> —Andy Warhol

Ian Rhys-Fitzsimmons: A Retrospective
New York, New York

The opening night of the retrospective at the Whitney Museum of American Art was jam-packed and I could not have been happier for Ian. Not only was he the first British artist to have a solo exhibition at the Whitney, he was one of the youngest living artists to have a major museum mount a retrospective exhibition of his work.

There were lines up and down Madison Avenue and crowds everywhere.

People swarmed and fawned and photographed Ian for hours, and Dick was right there at his side. I stayed in a different part of the room with Victor. It was wonderful to be with Victor again, watching him skillfully work a crowd that surely encompassed the entire art world. As I listened to him glad-hand (*Hi! Hi! Great to see you. Definitely. Of course, yes. Perfect!*), his complete fabulousness—for the very first time—didn't seem so out of reach to me. In the middle of the Whitney's crowded lobby, I felt like maybe nothing was so out of reach to me. A photographer's flash went off, and I looked across the room at Ian, graciously greeting his throng of adoring fans. Ian looked up just then, and our eyes met. He smiled at me and I was sure it was a different type of smile from the one he was giving everyone else. I smiled back, and his eyes seemed to sparkle just the tiniest bit more. Another photographer's flash went off, momentarily blinding Ian and causing him to look away. I smiled up at Victor, who smiled happily right back at me. It was clear to me then that when someone who once seemed godlike suddenly turns out to be human, it isn't always a bad thing. Sometimes, I realized, it just makes you love them more.

The morning after the opening, Ian called the gallery and told me he was knackered and was going to his farm in Connecticut and that he'd see me in a week. I wouldn't see him again until we left for Miami. I'd known I would see a lot less of him in New York and I'd known I was going to miss him; I just didn't know how much.

I didn't know that I would miss him so much that instead of going home one night, I walked to the Whitney Museum and stood across the street from it. I couldn't see Ian, away in Connecticut, and I couldn't see the sculptures inside the museum, but I felt a little less far away from him as I watched the Rhys-Fitzsimmons banner blowing in the wind. The longer I stood there, the closer I got to changing my mind about Ian and me not being meant to be. Maybe we were. *Maybe just not now,* I thought, as I crossed the street and began walking east, toward my apartment. *Maybe later.*

Being back at the Dick Reese Gallery was as unpleasant as I thought it would be. Having had the luxury of living in a world without Dick, being right in the middle of it all again was intolerable. I hated the sneering and the scowling, the whining and the hissing. I hated anything that had to do with him, but it was different now. Before, I had believed his behavior was something that had to be tolerated, something that had to be survived. I didn't think that anymore.

The day before we were leaving for Miami, Dick was in the midst of the breakdown to end all breakdowns. One of our lesser-known artists was defecting to another gallery. Though Dick never paid any attention to this artist and never gave him his own shows, Dick was beside, beside, beside himself that anyone could leave him. He intercommed me, hyperventilating, and told me to write a threatening letter to the artist. As Victor ran out for a banana juice, I could hear Dick screeching and whining and hissing upstairs, and I could hear the Velociraptor cooing and soothing him.

"Dick, Dick, what can I do? How can I help? What can I do to make it better?"

"Oh, Amanda. Well, I asked Jane to write a letter."

"Oh," said Amanda, forlorn, until I could hear the light bulb turning on over her head. "Jane must be so busy getting ready for the Miami Art Fair. Would you like me to write that letter instead?"

"Would you? That would be so helpful."

The Velociraptor tried intercomming me. I didn't answer. She could hop down the stairs on her Jurassic legs if she wanted to talk to me. I opened my drawer and took out a disk I had hidden behind my business cards. After looking first to make sure Clarissa was busy with whatever she was doing, I put the disk into the computer and printed out my résumé. I gathered up my "Art Fair Project: Miami" folder and although it was only two o'clock, I left the Dick Reese Gallery.

I walked down Tenth Avenue about four blocks and turned right.

The gallery was smaller than Dick Reese's, just one floor with all the desks off to the left side as you walked in. She was at one of the desks, radiating happiness and a better future, a world without Dick. Maybe it was just Susan Menton herself, but the entire gallery space seemed so sunny, so bright.

"Susan, hi," I said tentatively.

"Jane, how nice to see you. How are you?" she said warmly, a bit quizzically.

"I'm good," I said, my confidence growing with each minute. "How are you?"

"Oh, fine, fine. Busy, good."

"Good. I'm actually leaving tomorrow morning for the Miami Art Fair and then Ian has a show."

"Yes, I hear the Art Fair Project has been a great success. Ian deserves only that."

"He certainly does." I hesitated. "Susan, I'm here because I want to give this to you." I handed my résumé to her before I lost my nerve. She took it and smiled. After looking at it for a minute, she looked up at me.

"This looks very impressive," she said and smiled again. "When will you be back from Miami?"

"The first week in March."

"Let's talk as soon as you get back. I may be offering a new job to someone the first week in March," she said with a wink.

We both knew I shouldn't be there unless I wanted to leave Dick Reese right then, and I didn't. It would be crazy for me to quit right before going to Miami for a month. I couldn't wait to see Kate, and I couldn't leave Ian, not for the last part of his project. And the thought of not seeing him on the plane the next morning would just about kill me. I smiled back, we shook hands, and I told her I'd call her in March.

Instead of going back to the Dick Reese Gallery, I went to get a haircut.

35

JACK DAVIS, FORTUNE TELLER?

"If you look at something long enough, I've discovered the meaning goes away."
—Andy Warhol

I sat flipping happily through the February *Allure*, listening
to people check in for their hair appointments. I couldn't believe I'd done it. I couldn't believe that maybe as soon as
March I wouldn't work for Dick Reese anymore.

"I have a three o'clock with Martin. Daisy Crowe.
C-r-o-w-e."

Daisy Crowe? I started to feel cold. *Crowe with an 'e'?*

I sat frozen. I could see her at the reception desk; she
didn't have blond hair. She wasn't particularly tall. There
wasn't a lacrosse stick hanging out of her bag. She was wearing a coat, so I couldn't see if she was thin or fat. I didn't
want to know. I realized that in a minute she would turn

around and I would see her face. I didn't want to see her face.
Was she still with Jack? Was she happy to be with him or did
she constantly think, "Daisy, the way you get them is the way
you lose them"? Or maybe she wasn't anxious at all. Maybe
she was better with him than I was. Or worse yet, maybe he
was better with her. If she turned around, not only would I
see her face, I would also see her eyes. I would know if there
was happiness in them.

If I looked, I would know if he was a better man without me.

I got up and walked unannounced and unescorted in the
opposite direction of Daisy Crowe. I asked someone to wash
my hair. She looked confused and asked if my stylist was
ready for me. "He is," I answered, feeling strong. "And I
am, too."

"So, what are we going to do today?"

"Nothing major, just a trim. Like half an inch," I answered.

Anthony, my stylist, looked down at me. "I hate this long
hair on you. You are a beautiful girl. I want you to show your
face."

"I don't know, really . . ."

A foot was stamped. Not mine.

"I want you in shorter hair! " Anthony took a deep
breath and walked off, leaving me to consider.

Why, I wondered, *is he being so insistent?* Can he tell by
looking at me that everything has changed and he wants me

to have the proper, triumphant haircut to reflect my new inner beauty and strength?

Anthony returned. "You know I'm right, doll baby."

Or maybe he just wants to give a poor slob more than just a trim? It must be very frustrating to have someone tell you, No. Don't be creative. Don't be talented. Just a trim.

Anthony was waiting.

"Okay, Anthony." We smiled proudly at each other. "But just above my shoulders. I do *not* want chin length."

Momentarily his eyes lit up at the words *chin* and *length*, but I narrowed my own. Quickly recovering, he danced around as he arranged his scissors and started combing and clipping my hair into sections—joyously asking me to turn left, turn right, and look down, baby doll.

I filled Anthony in on the last months of my life, all the places I had been and all the things I had done. He told me it sounded like a wonderful experience, and I couldn't have agreed with him more. And then, before I knew it, he was finished.

My hair was smooth and blunt where before it had been uneven, shiny where it had been dull, and full where it had been lifeless. It was everything a girl could want from a haircut. I wanted to love it, but as I looked at myself in the mirror, what I *really*, really wanted was to cry. As I looked in the mirror at my almost-shoulder-length hair, all I saw was myself sitting next to Jack at the beach posing for a picture that would later sit on his dresser and then disappear.

"Baby? Don't you love it?" Anthony asked forlornly.

I couldn't answer him. I wanted to turn to the picture of

Jack that I saw next to me in the mirror and ask him the same question. "Didn't you love me?" It was a question I had asked him in my mind a million times. Now, six months later, I knew the answer. No.

No, he hadn't loved me.

He hadn't loved me the way I had hoped for.

Maybe he loved Daisy, but that wasn't for me to care about. I looked into the mirror again and saw only myself. It was true, what Jack had told me a lifetime ago. I *was* a better person and a stronger person. But he had been wrong in one respect. It wasn't because of him; no, I was a better and stronger person *in spite* of him. And looking closer into the mirror, I saw that my haircut was not at all like the haircut I had when I first met Jack. It was on an entirely different person.

"Anthony," I said at last. "I love it!"

36

REALLY, REALLY REDUX

"And then, my dear, it was like
a storybook fairytale."
—Andy Warhol

The next morning Ian came to the airport straight from Connecticut, so I didn't see him until right before we boarded the plane, at the gate. It was so good to see him. As we settled into our seats, Ian took out his ticket, checked something, smiled, and then looked over at me.

"Three hours," he said.

"Yeah," I said. It had been so long since I'd spent any real time with him, three hours didn't seem like nearly enough. "Just three." For the first time, I was a person who wanted to stay longer on a plane.

"Have you had your hair cut?" he asked me.

"I have," I said, happy he noticed.

"Well, it looks super."

"Not too short?" I asked.

"No. Jane, it looks super. Really."

"Thanks, Ian." I took the new *Art Forum* out of my bag, and noticed how handsome he looked on the cover, standing with his head slightly tilted to the side next to *Untitled: Gray*. A woman with long hair walked past us to the bathroom. I suddenly wanted hair like hers. I turned back to Ian. "See that girl? I like her hair. I want hair like that instead."

"No, Jane. It isn't my opinion that you would be better off with hair like that instead. I think your haircut looks smashing. I love your hair. I love you."

Oh. My. God.

His eyes suddenly got wider. That last part had slipped out. I didn't think he meant to say it. Yet he didn't look like he regretted it; he didn't look like a man who had just said something terribly wrong; he just looked startled.

Oh my God, did Ian Rhys-Fitzsimmons just say he loved me?

I wished, with all my wishing power: *Please don't let it be that he meant to add "r hair" to the end of "you." Please don't let it be that he actually meant to say "I love your hair" twice for emphasis. Please just let it be that he loves me.*

"What?" I whispered, guppy-eyed.

He seemed to internally straighten himself up, and he ran his hand over the side of his head, twice. Then he sat up straight, took a deep breath, and looked right at me.

"I love you, Jane."

I. Love. You. Jane.

"I have for a while now. I love your haircut, yes, but

that's not all. I love every last thing about you. I have loved working with you and traveling with you and getting to know what a beautiful person you are inside and out. I've loved everything about these art fairs because I've been at them with you. It's true, I hate flying and don't you see, for these past few months, every time I get on a plane, I hope it is a long flight because I know I will be sitting next to you."

He paused and smiled and we just stared at each other for a minute. He took a breath again, but not as nervous a breath as before, and then he took my hand.

"I look at you and I'm sure, as sure as I've ever been about anything, that with you I could fancy a love for life quite possible. Jane, you are my moors. You are my Rome."

I am his moors! I am his Rome!

"And I know you may not love me," he continued, "and that this is all terribly unprofessional and you very well could have me hauled off to the clink by one of those American sexual harassment lawyers."

I loved every single word he said right down to *harassment*. He said it *HA-rass-ment* rather than *ha-RASS-ment*. It sounded like a beautiful thing when he said it. I couldn't think straight; my stomach was zigging over and zagging back but it was a wonderful feeling. Ian loved me and had for a while! How could I not have known? But what about the PR bimbo he dated? I had a million questions I wanted to ask him and I had to start somewhere.

"But what about the PR bi—women you date?"

"I wouldn't call it dating. I have drinks and dinner with the PR women, but it has never been anything romantic. Jane," he said sweetly, "I am an artist, and a self-promoting artist at that. I need a good bit of PR as part of what I do, but it has always been strictly professional."

"Okay. Okay." I spoke slowly, trying to catch my breath. Breath. Breathy. I remembered Karina Kratsch. "And Karina? Do you date her?" I felt like the Barbara Walters special, but I wanted to know these things. I needed to know these things.

"Karina? Oh, good heavens, no!"

"But—"

"I know. I know. I do go to dinner with her quite frequently. Jane, now here is where I have perhaps not been completely honest with you." He looked at me seriously.

He hadn't been honest?

My smile fell and I think my heart actually started to hurt.

"No. Jane. Don't look so sad; it's not as awful as any of that. Karina is in no way anyone I would ever want to be with, even if I weren't hopelessly in love with you. She is not at all my type. But she is one phenomenal art dealer, with a first-rate gallery. The thing is, Jane, I don't care to be represented by Dick anymore. I think he is a horrible person, I hate the way he treats his staff, and I hate it, *hate* the way he treats you. And I don't think I am being immodest when I say that I don't feel he has done so very much to promote my career. I have done it on my own. Bloody hell, I'm even getting my own PR.

"So while we have been on the road, I have been going over some details with Karina about joining her gallery. Dick has made plenty of money on the Art Fair Project, much more than he laid out, so I feel we can part on honorable terms. I am going to tell him as soon as we get back from Miami."

I was so happy; I know it isn't right to be happy at the misfortune of another person, but it is probably okay to be happy at the misfortune of the minion of the antichrist. But more than that, I was *really,* really happy because *Ian Rhys-Fitzsimmons said he was hopelessly in love with me!* "This is all so incredible. . . . Ian, how come you didn't tell me—"

"Well, there was that tall Texan chap you seemed to need some time to recover from, and I wanted you to have that time. And then there was that bloke from Chicago and the— I don't very well know anymore. I should have said something. I don't know why I didn't."

"No. Thank you. Thank you for giving me that time. I needed it, and you told me everything now, and you love me, and that's all that matters."

He leaned over and kissed me then.

It was the best first kiss ever. I knew right then that I would be okay if I never had a first kiss with anyone else. I was ready to move on to all the rest of it: to all the things that people tell you about when they tell you about really being in love. I was ready to do it all with Ian. I couldn't wait to tell him that I loved him. I couldn't wait to tell him that every day. But first, I had to ask one more question. "Ian?"

"Yes."

"I was wondering, when we land in Miami . . ."

"Yes?" he asked and smiled at me. I smiled back and I felt as if I might smile forever.

"Would you like to come to dinner at my friend Kate's house?"

"Jane," he said, "I would *really,* really love to."

". . . she's very happy now."

—Andy Warhol